DARLING

NEVER EVER NEVERLAND

K.T. HANNA

AMARANTHINE PRESS

ISBN

Ebook: 978-1-948983-04-4

Paperback: 978-1-948983-03-7

Nick
Without whom, Darling wouldn't have made it

FOREWORD

this book contains scenes that may be disturbing for some readers

TEA

*E*ven as David and I slip from the shadows of the causeway, I know Neverland will bring him the peace he deserves.

"Wendy?" His voice is mouse-like, as is his nose. It twitches when he's excited, like now.

"Yes?" I smile for his benefit as I scan the streets.

On the corner of Whitehorse and Matlock the guard are changing, which is good, because they'll be less inclined to notice us. Another street later, two lamplighters wait for the dusk's approach and I hear Big Ben's chimes faintly in the distance. It's later than I anticipated, and far later than I intended. Mother will not be pleased.

"Is it really real?"

David's soft voice pulls me back. He reminds me of my brothers, both waiting for me at home, because they have a home to wait in. His small face is pale, and his beady eyes shine with an eagerness I understand all too well. I'd stop for a moment if time weren't of the essence. Instead, I squeeze his tiny fingers with what I hope is reassurance and smile down at him.

"It's real, David. In Neverland, you'll never have to grow up."

His whole face lights up with relief and purpose. "When we asked if it was real, I never thought it were, Wendy. But the way you spoke..."

I pat the back of his hand with a finger this time, trying to be reassuring. He's been housed at the boy's orphanage in Stepney Causeway for the last few years. Been made a scapegoat, punished, and locked down in the dank cellars when he wouldn't steal what he was told to. He's younger than John, and I feel a pang every time I remember how much adults don't listen to the problems of the boys there.

A shadow falls across our path and my thoughts scatter as I stop abruptly, pulling David closer. The tremor running through his frail body echoes into my hand, and indignation rises in my throat to berate whoever has scared him.

"Sorry, miss." The old man tips his hat awkwardly, a slight wobble to his step as he continues on. A faint waft of brandy, like father drinks sometimes, drifts back to us, and I crinkle my nose, waiting until his footsteps fade.

"It'll be all right, David. Don't you worry. We'll get you there, safe and sound."

"Thomas said you would." David nods, gripping my hand tighter as we move on.

It's strange how overwhelmingly dark the house is as we approach it, despite the sun still sitting low in the sky. Its Tudor eaves cast deceptively deep shadows, and the criss-cross windows act as foreboding bars to keep people out. When I glance down at David as I lead him around to the back, he's biting his lip and staring at the steeple of Dunstan's church visible over the partition wall. The door through to the kitchen is always unlocked, just a little stubborn and I have to let his hand go in order to push our way in.

"In here?" he gulps.

I nod and can't fault him for sounding scared. The house has been empty for longer than my father's bank cares to admit. And they say eavesdropping never brings any good. If I hadn't listened to Father's conversation, I'd never have found the perfect way-house. I wanted to bring them through my house, to have Tinkerbell and Peter meet us there. But my common sense won out. Mother would never let me bring so many boys to our house—she doesn't know anything about

Neverland. Even if we told her, like most adults, I'm sure she wouldn't believe us.

With the light fading outside, the inside is darker than I'm used to. We can't use the candles until we reach the cellar.

"Not much longer," I murmur to David.

His grip has transferred to the lovely navy overcoat of the dress mother insisted I wear today. It brings out my eyes, she said. I wanted to tell her it was crushing my torso, but I didn't have the courage to complain. These things cost a fortune.

It's a shame we can't wait upstairs for the duration, but there'd be no light. The stairs that sweep through the living area are beautiful. A far cry more grandiose than the ones in my father's home. These twist around with beautifully-carved banisters and what would once have been shining wooden boards. The chandelier that dominates the room hangs precariously above us, its crystals dim with grime gathered over the years.

David stares wistfully at the staircase and the promising arch window at the top of it, but I tug his hand and pull him gently toward the closed door of the basement.

Once down there though, I light one of the several candles I have scattered. As the room brightens his shoulders soften, and relief spreads across his face. I did my best to make it cozy down here after the first time, despite the rat I saw scurrying about. The boys need to wait until the tea sets in; not everyone has a head for flying.

"Here." I say, gesturing to one of the cushion piles. "Sit down, and I'll make you some tea."

David jumps on the cushions with glee and smiles up at me before succumbing to a horrible and lingering cough he's had since his last visit to the cellars of the orphanage. His soft brown eyes reflect the candlelight as he finally speaks.

"Thanks for this, Wendy. I reckon I'd get awful sick next time. Do you know what they made us do?"

I nod my head slowly, recalling the horror stories Thomas told me. When he was younger, Thomas too, was subjected to this. Some of the home employees and volunteers use the boys to pickpocket and steal, to smuggle stolen goods to the parks for drop off. They're already in a home, but too many "reported incidents" to keep them in line result in being shipped overseas to a colony, if they survive their punishment times in the cellars. A tear rolls down my cheek and I hurriedly wipe it away. David doesn't need to see me cry, I'm supposed to be saving him. And I will. Peter will.

His tiny hand pats my own awkwardly, followed by a brief and impulsive hug. "Don't be sad, Wendy. It'll all be a'right now."

I laugh as I sprinkle the tea leaves into the strainer and set about lighting the little stove. It won't be lit long enough to smoke us out down here, just long enough to boil a cup of tea. David is such a positive soul, I can't imagine why the adults won't believe these boys. Maybe they all get a cut, maybe they're all corrupt. If I think about it too long, I'll get angry again.

"Yes, it will." I murmur, knowing he wants some sort of answer from me.

I glance at the dimming light through the slit-windows high up in the brick of the cellar and frown. Mother won't be impressed. She rarely is with me since she moved me out of the nursery. It's not my fault; I never asked to be moved.

"Can you tell me more about Neverland?" David's tone is so hopeful that it saps my irritation.

"I've told you all our adventures, David. There's not much else I can tell you." I say the words gently knowing he wants to know everything. As his smile fades slightly, I hurry to add, "But now you'll get to experience your own adventures. You won't need me to tell you."

He nods his head emphatically. "Do I really get to fly?"

"High in the sky. Second star to the right, and straight on until morning."

The tea is ready and I mix his cup before heading over and bending down to hand it to him. Its pungent smell wafts up to reach me as I ruffle his hair while he takes his first sip and grimaces. "That's really sweet. What's it for again?"

"Helps you relax so you don't get too anxious. Can't get pixie dust to work on you if you're too worked up to concentrate now, can we?"

His eyes light up and he gulps the tea down so fast I can see his pupils enlarge, and the tension drains from his shoulders as the tea begins to work.

"Now all we have to do is wait." I answer and stand back up, brushing off my skirts.

He grins and his shoulders sag a little more, further tension leaking out of them. He's almost ready to go, which is good, because I think they'll be here shortly and I really have to get home. Peter isn't usually here this early, but I can't come out after dark tonight, and we had to get David out today. There's a creak behind me and I swirl around, suddenly paranoid that someone followed me. I look a lot more grown up than I feel in these silly dresses. But it's just Peter, standing by the coal cellar door. He has that typical smirk on and with a tilt of his hat, it grows into a smile.

"Miss Darling." He twirls around and bows, his feet inches from the floor, a twinkle in his eye, and exaggerated hand flourishes.

Laughter bubbles at the back of my throat even though this mildly sarcastic edge of his mocks me for coming back to my parents. Yet, he still comes when I ask, so I ignore it, even if it worries me slightly.

"I can't come tonight," I say, and wish it were otherwise. "I'm late, and mother will be upset with me."

I'm not sure if I imagine it or not, but Peter's smile droops for a moment before he shrugs. "Can't have mother Darling upset now, can we?"

A shiver runs down my spine at the faint spark in Peter's eyes. It's gone as quickly as it appeared. It must have been the candles reflecting off the steel door. I'm sure of it.

Then Peter smiles, and I remember the cheeky, fun-loving boy who literally swept me off my feet. "Don't worry. We know where you are, Wendy. We'll take good care of...?"

"Oh." Silly me, where are my manners? Peter always flusters me. "This is David. And David," I say taking his hand and offering it to Peter. "This is Peter Pan."

*A*ll too suddenly I'm home. It's quiet, and what's left of the sunlight doesn't make it through the frosted glass of the porch windows. The evening chill begins to creep into my bones and heart. I know mother and father love us, but this house feels so impersonal. Ever since they made me leave the nursery, little by little, warmth leaks out through the floorboards and leaves me struggling to find heat.

"Wendy Darling!" Mother's voice is sharp as she addresses me from the door to the sitting rooms.

"Sorry, Mother." I can't bring myself to meet her eyes.

I know how they look, I've seen them so many times. The way the skin will crinkle around her mouth, turning down without frowning. How the crow's feet at the edges of her eyes suddenly appear just long enough to help her air that disappointment in me, of not knowing what to do with a daughter who just won't heed.

I see the shadow before I see the woman it belongs to. My mother's forced smile should have been enough to warn me that she had company. Our guest's golden hair is so shiny, it's almost blinding. Piercing blue eyes regard me, smiling just like the perfect upturned mouth they belong to. I curtsy clumsily.

"My apologies Mrs. Davenport, I didn't realize we had company."

"Nonsense, Wendy. I popped over to arrange dinner with your mother." She looks me up and down, a strangely pleased smile creasing her lips. "You're blossoming into a beautiful young lady. I hear you volunteer now?"

I nod my head, suddenly uncomfortable. Mrs. Davenport has always had this unattainable beauty. We did many things with their family when Father first started working for the bank. Come to think of it, I haven't had the displeasure of seeing their son since Neverland. Aldon, Albert...something like that. Right little piece of work, he was. Torturing beetles in his mother's garden. Throwing rocks to see if his puppy could dodge them. It's difficult to suppress the shudder that runs down my back at the memories that surface as she speaks to me. "I do, at the boys' home with Mother."

"Excellent." She moves closer, turning to my mother before speaking. "Then tomorrow it is, dear?"

Mother nods. "I can't wait to catch up. We've all been so busy."

She's using that smile. The fake one. The one she uses with people she feels she has to impress. I'll never understand adults.

"Then until tomorrow." Mrs. Davenport turns back to me, briefly laying a hand on my shoulder. "I look forward to tomorrow, Wendy. I've been waiting so long for this."

I jump slightly as Joan closes the door behind her, not having noticed when our maid entered the room, and not understanding what the woman is talking about. "Mother, the Davenports are coming for dinner tomorrow?"

Mother nods, watching shadows through the glass as her guest climbs into a carriage.

"Why?" I venture.

She turns to me, a frown tugging at her lips. "To eat, of course. We shall have supper at six-thirty sharp, Wendy. You need to have time to wash and dress. Whatever you do, please, don't be late tomorrow. It's a very important day for all of us."

This time I look up, her eyes have very slight wrinkles around the edges, and I wonder if maybe they'll mirror what mine will look like someday. She managed to step around my question. What could be so important for all of us? For Father, perhaps, and by extension Mother. Sometimes I wonder if the lost boys truly ever understood what it was they have. At the time I thought they were crazy for not having parents, but since moving to my own room, I have a greater appreciation for the freedom I now so sorely miss.

"I won't be late tomorrow. I'll be on time." I try to appease her, and keep my tone smooth.

"Be early. You have to put on your best evening dress and make sure your hair is perfect. Be well rested. Don't go walking the long way home. I know you love the church gardens, Wendy, but there's a time for everything. Tomorrow is not it." She turns and walks away, tugging at the skirts she's almost as unaccustomed to wearing as I am.

I wish she still wore aprons. Mother does bake the best apple tart.

I blink as the light streaming through the front door changes and wonder just how long I've been standing here reminiscing about how good the apple tart used to taste when I was younger. The stairs seem endless this evening as I trudge up them, uneasiness heavy in my stomach, like a stone.

I sit down on my bed and begin peeling off the layers that make this dress. It doesn't feel like my room, everything is foreign, except for that lamp. Mother loves blue. She says it brings out our eyes. And so these walls are blue and white—or periwinkle, I think she said. As if that beautiful name will make me forget that as an adult nothing I want seems to matter. I don't understand how the human race exists. Why on earth do people want to grow up? I don't want to stop listening to important things. I don't want to doubt what I've believed in as a child. And I don't want to hold anyone's life in my hands and do the wrong thing.

Even the porcelain roses on this lamp that grandmother gave me for my tenth birthday seem to have aged. They mock me from their frozen perch. *We all age,* they whisper to me, *you will age too, just as we have, gather dust and be discarded to the next generation.* I glance at my aging body in the full-length glass on the front of my wardrobe. I'm turning into a woman. Developing, as mother calls it. The visage is still distant from my mind, like I can't register that it's actually my own reflection. I open the door, and the image flees as I pick out the pale pink dinner dress. It's mother's favorite, because it accents my golden-brown hair. I'm still not sure how I feel about it.

Tiger Lily wouldn't be caught and trussed in something like this. Not that it should matter. The lost boys have it so good. I want to go back. It's the only thing I'll ever want. It's also probably the only thing I can never have. As much as I might want to drop everything and travel there. I'm not unlucky like the homeless boys. My family is here, in this house, all of us. A mother, a father, and my brothers. How could I leave them? They'd worry, or at the very least, they'd not understand.

As if thinking of them summons one, my door inches open as a hand gripping a teddy bear pushes it inward, followed shortly by a head with tousled hair.

"Wendy?" Michael says, in that pudgy-cheeked way. "You come down to dinner wif' us?"

I smile at his continuing trouble with a t and h and scoop him up in my arms. He's getting heavier. Older, too. I wish I could save them from growing up as well. Instead, I snuggle his fat little cheeks, and he laughs. It's a silvery waterfall with not a care in the world, and the smile it brings to my face remembers how it was to laugh like that.

"Of course I'm coming to dinner. I'm ravenous!"

VOLUNTEERS

I trail my fingers over the heavy curtains drawn across the windows in the dining room. They're there to give us privacy and stop the boys from looking outside and becoming distracted instead of eating. As I sit down, the table seems vast and bulky, with huge, velvet-seated, wooden-backed chairs. Everyone in this room is so far away. I remember dinners in a much fonder light when I was their age, before I had to get dressed up for them, and before Father changed.

After Neverland, Father's shadow became trickier than Peter's. The jolly face with the welcoming arms for me is missing, and in its place is this man. He's like a darker version of himself, lurking at the end of the table every night, not caring that he is about to take away what childhood I might have left.

"Wendy!" Johnathan's voice tears me out of my contemplations.

I've barely touched a morsel on my plate, and I can tell as I bite into the Brussels sprout on my fork that everything is at best luke-warm now. It was piping hot a moment ago.

"Don't yell at the dinner table," my mother chides him gently as she goes over a list to the side of her.

She's barely looking at any of us. Father is rustling through the morning paper I know he didn't have time to read before he dashed out of the house to begin his long working day at the bank. Really, what does he do all day at a bank?

Johnathan looks sheepish for a moment before grinning. His huge glasses magnify that innocent look. All of a sudden I want to protect him from all the bad things in this world, but most of all from growing up. Maybe he should go to Neverland. Then again, for the same reasons I can't, that's probably not the best idea. As much as Mother and Father seem distant these days, they don't deserve to lose their children and never find them again, do they?

"Mother." Michael pipes up.

Every time I look at him all I see is this roly-poly bundle of huggable love. He smiles up at me when he calls Mother's name, a shine to his expression. I've been around more than our parents for most of his life, and sometimes I think he realizes it too.

"Yes dear?" she asks, not really paying attention.

"Can Wendy tuck us in tonight?"

This time she looks up and a smile softens her face, momentarily bringing back the woman I remember so fondly. "Of course she can, if you ask her nicely."

For a second there is this understanding between us. Maybe she realizes I hate letting go. It could just be wishful thinking on my behalf, but I don't mind if it is.

"Will you, Wendy?" Michael's lower lip trembles and he casts his gaze down. It's the classic puppy dog look he learned so expertly from Nanna.

"Of course I will." A smile tugs at my lips involuntarily and warm happiness spreads through me.

My brothers need me, much like the lost boys did, and the boys at home need me now. Maybe that's why I don't want to take my brothers with me. I don't want to hand them over to Peter. If I lost Michael and John, it would be even lonelier here.

And Nanna? Nanna would miss them. She's just a dog, but she helped raise us when we were tiny and unable to afford real help. As silly as that sounds, she was an amazing babysitter. Protective and loyal, now she gets to sit by the fire and live out her days as well rewarded as she should.

Before following my brothers up, I walk over and crouch down carefully so as not to crumple my dress. Out of the corner of my eye I notice that Mother nods approvingly before venturing into the kitchen with a briefly passing kiss on the top of my father's head, and ushering in our maid who's only here during the day. Personally, I think Mother was about to clear the table, but remembered when she got into the kitchen that she no longer has to.

"Who's a good girl?" I say softly, reaching out a hand to scratch Nanna in that perfect spot just behind her ears.

She looks up at me, tongue lolling out the side of her mouth and gives me that unmistakable Nanna smile. I'd throw my arms around her and hug her if it was even remotely ladylike and my mother hadn't just walked back into the room. Instead, I stand up, kiss Father's head, and briefly squeeze Mother's shoulders, before murmuring good night and heading up the stairs.

I know what the boys want, and I can't blame them. They are boys, after all. And who doesn't love a good pirate tale or three? I wonder what it would take for Father to pin all his hopes on the boys instead of whatever it is my parents have in store for me. Michael and John have a future here, even if that means they have to grow up. But those poor boys in the Causeway? The only place they will ever be free is Neverland. I have to help as many as I can. They can't live like that— no one should have to!

My hand rests above the doorknob as I stand outside the nursery door listening to them throw pillows at each other and hop around from bed to bed, giggling amongst themselves. Not long ago I was in that room too, and while it bothered me at the time, I'd give almost anything to go back. I miss the warmth, the love, the pure happiness they exude. I've seen how amazing staying young can be, how freeing never growing up is. These last few months make me wish I could stop time.

With a deep breath, and a shake of my head, I push the door open. "Now, who wants to hear about a pirate cove and treasure?"

"Me!"

"No, me!"

I fend off a pillow that narrowly misses my head and do my best to appear stern, but John's laughter puts an end to that. "I can't tell you stories if you beat me up with pillows!"

Which, of course, is the wrong thing to say. Two pillows hit me simultaneously, from each side. I can't help but laugh with them.

"Just you wait," I say as sternly as I can and start chasing them.

Johnathan fends me off with his wooden sword.

"Ye'll not take me, scurvy scum!" He shouts, brandishing his weapon and another pillow as a shield.

I pick up the closest thing to me, a lid of some sort, and hold it out like a shield. "Try and stop me, matey!"

I think my accent needs some work, but none of us care.

Michael is fending us off with Teddy, as he clumsily flounces a blanket over the foot of his bed and a hastily-gathered chair.

"Beware 'de bear!" he shouts and retreats in his cave intermittently growling.

Both John and I look at each other, stifling our laughter behind big grins. I put my finger to my lips, motioning him to be quiet, and we tiptoe toward the makeshift cave one slow step at a time.

The constant growling almost undoes me, but we narrow in on the dangerous bear. When suddenly it leaps out and jumps at us, growling ferociously. Michael's teddy attacks us both and we go down.

"No!" I cry, feebly waving my lid about.

"Help. Please," John wails, theatrically dropping his sword and stumbling to the ground.

For a few precious moments, we've found a niche in time.

Michael giggles so hard he falls over on his bed, and I lift him up, ticking his stomach until he gasps for air. "Stop. Enough. Wendy. Please!"

I mock-glare at Johnathan, and he backs up, hands in front of his face as if fending me off. "I yield. I yield!"

With a grin, I set Michael back on his bed and let him snuggle with his pillow against my side. "It's time to sit and hear a tale of a pirate who lost his hand, and replaced it with..." I pause, but only briefly as they chime in chorus.

"A hook! Captain Hook!"

Their faces shine with eagerness that never fails to bring a smile to my face. My brothers are so much more real than the girls Mother's tried to introduce me to. I'll do anything to protect my brothers. Anything.

~

*I*t's late spring, and Mother insists that pale green suits me well. I don't mind *that* so much. But these hats? Whoever thought such huge things were a good idea should really try to wear one for an extended period of time. This day dress is pale with darker green stripes, comes together in an empress line just under the bust to splay outwards in an A-line skirt. At least it's lighter than the one I wore yesterday.

"Wendy! Wendy!" Michael runs around the dining table, teddy dragging behind him as his little cheeks turn ruddy with exertion. He loves to push the few boundaries he has when Father isn't here.

"Now, Michael," I chide him gently, scooping him up and seating him on the cushioned chair so he can peer over the top. "Your tutor will be here shortly."

For a few moments I'm back in the nursery, leafing through brightly-colored books full of words and wisdom. I shake my head and try to reinforce my smile. Learning about faraway places, plays, history and writing—all of those things—made Neverland such a beautiful memory.

"He's supposed to start his letters today." John's tone is serious, like he mostly is—each word carefully chosen before it's spoken.

"That explains it." It truly does.

I watch Michael wriggle around on his chair, eyes bright and full of excitement for the day ahead. For that brief moment, I wish none of us had to grow up and step into such a repetitive routine. Sleep to breakfast, work to home, dinner to bed. Bitterness sinks like lead in my lungs, and for a moment breathing is difficult. I remember the plank, the walking, and the drop...

Until Mother's voice breaks the spell.

I try not to gasp as I blink up at her.

"Sorry, Mother?" Air rushes back into my lungs and the vision breaks as the memory fades.

"Really, Wendy. Where has your head been all morning? Try to pay more attention. We're going to be late. You'll just have to sneak a bun on the way." She pats the back of my chair, urging me to get up. I'm not sure where the time went, because the boys have already left the room.

Mother ushers me out of the house with her for our daily routine. On these walks from Whitehorse onto the commercial lane, I see the mother I've always known and loved. This rosy glow enters her cheeks, and her eyes shine with an enthusiasm I remember from years ago. I know she used to worry about money and affording us all, but now she worries about appearances and how we are perceived by others. Another reason I don't understand adults. When I turn sixteen next year, will I suddenly forget all the things I used to enjoy?

Horse-drawn carriages are still plentiful, and they're beautiful. I love the smell of those animals, though their sheer size causes me to keep my distance. But lately, over the last few years, mechanical, horseless carriages have become all the rage.

More and more people have them. They're not only a status symbol, but a mark of how far technology is changing the world. Remarkable really, that we can replace a beast that has borne us forever. I wonder what else we'll replace.

Some motorized carriages pass us as we walk along the lane toward our turn off for Stepney Causeway. Mother waves at someone, and the smile affixed to her face is no longer real but the one I despise instead. It'd suit me fine to give up everything we have if it just meant I got her back again.

I pick my way across the street, slightly trailing Mother. The one good thing about mechanical carriages is their lack of horse manure.

I'm sure they'll catch on if only to avoid stepping in excrement all the time.

The path we walk down to get to the causeway doesn't have a name, but it does have an overhang. It towers above us, hanging precariously, judging those who walk beneath it for something I'm too scared to contemplate. Its shadows reach into corners and crevices like fingers waiting to catch someone unaware. I can't help but feel a sense of awe every time I see the row of houses that makes up the Stepney Boys' Home.

Several stories high and made of brick, the windows are surrounded by stark whitewash, which only serves to highlight the age-old grime accumulating on the panes. Each building shoulders onto another and looms over those who pass below. In the cold moments of morning, the chimneys out puff their smoke. It lingers for a few moments, blanketing the area in a dank and smoggy mantle.

They've been homes for years as far as I know, and Mother likes to spend her mornings bringing them freshly-baked bread to help give these boys some sustenance. We volunteer now because that's what banker's wives do. Even though I've been here with Mother many times since I left the nursery, my courage always fades and holds my tongue in the presence of the other adults. They're so big and so busy, and their skin is so rough their lies stick to it like grease on a pan.

Mrs. Johnson is always happy to see me, happy to see us. Or at least the wrinkles and tiredness around her eyes decreases momentarily when she sees us. I assume that means she's happy. Today she takes the bread basket from my mother and ushers us to help with lunch preparation for the boys. Pulling a slightly tattered blue apron over my green dress I cringe for a moment. I'm sure Mother told me never to wear those two colors together, but I kind of like them. I see a trend of loving things Mother doesn't.

Buttering the bread is easy, and it won't take me long. The kitchen counters are old and wooden, with an age of knife strokes that have their own tales. What I love most though is what I get to do after I've finished that. While Mother converses with the other adults and even sometimes leaves to go home, I get to go and read to the little boys who live here. There are so many of them, dressed in coarse material that must scratch more than the silly embroidery on my dresses. Their faces have sunken cheeks and eyes that are constantly haunted. I wish I didn't know the source of some of their woe. The conditions in this home aren't ideal—always a charity, they should never live under the threat of adults they thought they could trust.

I glance around the kitchen warily, trying to ferret out who might be one of the ringers who use the boys. But everyone in here is busy, not a mote of attention for anything else. I'd be inclined to disbelieve the tales if I hadn't seen the bruisings myself, or how gaunt a boy was when he returned from solitary punishment. There has to be a way to get more of them to Neverland and away from this hell.

THOMAS

Armed with a new fairy tale, I march out of the kitchen.

Bright eyes greet me, lighting up the otherwise drab room. Carpets that lost their colors years ago barely cover the stone floor and do little to lend any warmth. Even now the once heavy slabs of material are worn and threadbare in most visible places. The boys don't seem to mind though. They have chairs and the occasional rough wooden table to hang off. Monkeys, the lot of them. So much like the lost boys.

Hugging the book in my arms, I walk to the chair they've left vacant for me. In their somber dark-colored shorts and vests, they huddle at my feet. Their ages range from tiny four-year-olds through to boys around ten to twelve. Only a few around my age remain, mostly to help shepherd the younger ones about. As I flip the book open, the boys call out.

"No. Wendy! Tell us more about Neverland!"

I glance around as I look up at them, making sure there are no adults present. They won't listen to what's happening right in front of them, but they'd put a stop to tales of Neverland in no time. Tybalt, a cheeky nine-year-old, grins at me from his perch on a table to the right. I stare at him a little longer, because I haven't seen him for a few days. Those flushed cheeks are more hollow than usual, and as he moves, I spy bruises around the collar of his shirt. It would have to be him. He's so fragile, so tiny. Like all the others, I just want to smuggle him away and set him free.

"Tybalt. You know better than that," I admonish him.

They all know Neverland is taboo around the adults. Every one of them grins in conspiracy with me, and for a moment we're around a campfire, dancing, throwing food, singing. But it's gone the next time I blink and they're back here in this drab existence.

"Not fair, Wendy." Tybalt's pout sets in on his face as he scrunches his lips deliberately. "You can't tell us about them lost boys and not give us more."

There's a twinkle in his eyes that rarely leaves, and his personality shines through like a sunny day. Even after being forced into the thieving circle, punished and deprived of food, Tybalt still has smiles to spare. If Michael *has* to grow up, I want him to have that much faith in the world too.

I sigh and close the book in my hands, keeping an eye on the dining room door.

"Well, then," I say, and the whole room heaves a collective gasp.

Some of their faces are smudged with the dirt prevalent throughout the orphanage, others have serviceable but threadbare clothes, pulled tightly around them to fend of the breeze in this sometimes drafty room. They clench their hands with excitement, mouths slightly open, and wait for me to speak, to cling to my every word.

It's such a mean world that puts adults who don't care about them in charge of their well-being. My stomach burns for a moment and I want, more than anything, to stop this, to help them. Maybe it's because I know I can. Maybe I've only helped two so far, but it's just the beginning.

They lean forward as a group, ever so slowly. The movement snaps me out of my thoughts and I let myself smile. Telling them more about that place will only help keep it in my memory, and maybe then, I won't have to grow up so quickly either. But just as I'm about to speak, a shadow falls across the doorway and I hesitate, a sudden lump in my throat.

"Wendy." It's Mother, and I can't help the plethora of emotions that run through to punch me in the stomach as I realize she's still trying to pull me toward adulthood.

"Yes, Mother?" I try to keep my voice steady, my tone polite, like the good daughter she so needs me to be.

"I have to go home to begin preparations for tonight. Come along after you finish the story so you won't be late." Her tone is demure, but I can hear steely undertones just for me and my tardiness.

That's all right, though. She does have a point.

"Of course. I'll be there."

The whole room lets out a sigh of relief once the door to the kitchen closes.

"Well, that's a relief, 'innit." Tybalt's cheery voice rips me back to the room full of waiting boys still eagerly leaning forward. "Thought she was gonna take you with her. Been waiting for a Neverland story for days!"

I blink at him and suddenly laugh. It suffuses me, through my head, down to the tips of my toes and for a few moments I forget the constant dread that haunts this home.

"Tell us, Wendy." This voice is smoother, a little deeper than the younger ones surrounding me, and I've come to know it so well. I scan the room as he continues to speak, trying to pick out where he's hiding this time.

"Tell us another tale of Neverland, that we might never grow up too?"

Finally, in a corner to my back left, I find him. Standing in the shadow of the door to the first set of sleeping rooms, he's taller than Peter, but has similar orange hair. His face isn't triangular, and its edges are softer, sweeter, just like his disposition and how he can always make me laugh. His eyes bore into me with their usual intensity and the reason why I don't want to go home early hits in the pit of my stomach like good French toast. I look forward to him being here. Thomas always steps in when the boys get out of hand, not that they mean to, but he can always set them straight without ruffling feathers. He's the big brother to them all, and sometimes so much more to me. Whenever he's around, I feel peaceful and safe.

"Thomas." Even his name is easy to say. He's the one actual friend I've made here, the one who realized my tales weren't just tales.

I don't have many female friends, though to her credit, Mother has tried. Their conversation always seems so frivolous and petty. I prefer the company of my brothers, of the boys here, and especially of Thomas. He suggested Neverland for the others. He asked for James. He asked for David. But he's never asked me to take him, and part of me hopes he never does.

Thomas saunters closer, with that same staggered step Peter favors. Some of their similarities are striking. Thomas sits near, but not quite close, letting the little ones push forward to be close to the tale weaver.

"Regale us," he says in his voice, the timbre of which I could listen to forever.

It always makes me wonder where he came from. Maybe he's a Neverland spy and that's why he believed me in the first place.

Shaking my head, I grip the book against my chest to ground myself. Sometimes my imagination runs off with me, usually to Neverland. I take a deep breath and begin the story. This time I'll tell them one of my favorites. A tale of pirates and clocks, of hooks and crocodiles, of swords and faeries, of flight and feasts, and of course, as always—of the lost boys who never grow up.

The boys are usually fed in stages so not everyone is crammed at the serving tables at once. They take the youngest ones in first and filter methodically through by age. This usually results in Thomas being one of the last to be fed, and in turn, the one who lingers in the room with me.

I'm not certain how old he is, but he appears to be around my age, perhaps somewhat younger. Is it as rude to ask a boy his age as it is apparently a girl? These are the etiquette things that confuse me, to my mother's complete exasperation.

"Wendy?" Thomas's voice pulls me away from whatever thoughts I was about to have. It doesn't matter what I'm thinking or doing when he speaks to me, I'll always hear him.

"Sorry." I attempt a smile, but I'm a little worried about the meeting this evening, about the Davenports and the apparent importance of my being there.

It's never been important for me to be at a dinner in my life. Usually the children are hidden upstairs in the nursery with Nanna or a tutor depending on time of day. Mrs. Davenport seems nice enough, if memory serves me well. After all, I've known her as long as I can remember. Why would she be looking forward to it?

"What's this thing you have tonight?" he asks, interrupting my thoughts again.

"I'm not sure. Father's boss and his wife are coming to visit. For supper, I believe."

"Important guests?" he asks and steps closer.

Here, I can see the green in his eyes, and it sparkles so differently from Peter's. Thomas has strength not born of flight or magic, but of weathering time that's only been cruel and difficult. The boys need him here, to look out for them and step in if things get too bad. That's what I tell myself anyway. Neverland doesn't need Thomas.

Instead of answering directly, I shrug and move away, a sudden chill stealing through my sundress. There's always something my parents aren't telling me. I wish they'd make up their minds. *Grow up, Wendy, but we still won't tell you anything, because you're a child.*

"Probably something to do with Father's work."

"Ah." Thomas plops himself down on one of the rickety tables and grins. "I thought you were going to Neverland without me again."

"I don't actually go." Even as I say the words defensively, I know he didn't mean it like that.

Still, it irks me that I haven't been back, that the only contact I have is fleeting, barely tangible. Even when Peter's here I feel like he's speaking in riddles, goading me, daring me to come with him again.

And Tinkerbell never offers me the dust. All I want to do is be there, to fly to the second star on the right, and go straight on until the sun rises over the beauty of Neverland. But the option is never brought up. The closest I get now is taking these boys away. But last night was dangerous.

"Hey." Thomas's brow is pinched, and he shakes his head. "I didn't mean anything by that. I know you don't go. You're a delivery service. Sorta stork-like, but with grown boys."

He winks at me and suddenly I'm back at ease and the chill is gone.

"Sorta," I say, the colloquialism strange on my tongue. "Neverland delivery, ready for pick up. Where you never have to grow up." I say the words softly, because the louder they are, the more real it is, and the harsher the reality we're all stuck in becomes.

"Cheer up." Thomas claps me on the shoulder. "You've done good work here. The boys' spirits are much better now."

"Do they miss David?" I whisper, not sure if I should be saying his name out loud. Surely those who audit and monitor this place will know boys have started to go missing. I wish whoever it was would look deeper and find out why.

"They all just know he's safe now." Thomas's smile lights up his face and makes my heart slow a little.

"Good then. Here's to not getting caught."

Thomas brushes his hands through his hair, and for a moment any resemblance to Peter is lost. It's like a brief burst of color overlaying the otherwise dim room, but it's gone in a heartbeat and I'm quite certain my mind is just being overactive.

"Think Neverland will ever fill up?"

It's not a question I've thought about before, so it takes me by surprise. "I'm not sure. There should be room enough for plenty."

And then I realize how desperately Thomas wants to go. The boys need him here. He can't go. And most of all, he can't leave me here alone.

"Ah," he says, and for once his eyes don't meet mine. Instead, he looks at the ground and scuffs his feet against the floor visible through the carpet.

"I'm here," I say, and wish it were enough. "Even if I can't actually be here all the time. The boys need someone to look out for them. Someone who believes what they say."

Thomas grins again. "True." But I can hear the frustration no matter how he tries to hide it. "Can't help them live forever without you."

I smile back and glance at the clock next to the dining room doorway. "Oh no," I murmur. "The time."

He glances up too and then gestures at my dress. "Can you run in that?"

"I guess I'll find out." I'm already halfway out the room.

PLANS

*A*fter practically running a few blocks, even these lightweight skirts weigh heavily against my frame. My boots pinch at my toes, and I wish the laces on them would burst and leave me barefoot to run the rest of the way. But the dress doesn't get lighter, and my feet aren't magically granted freedom from their new constrictive home.

I stop at the iron gate to our property, just the White Horse Lane side of the main road, and gather my energy. Though I'm decidedly warmer than I'd like to be, I'm quite certain Mother won't be upset with me for being late. Gathering myself, I take a deep breath and head up the stairs to the front door.

"Wendy Darling!"

It would seem I was incorrect. Mother can scold me about anything.

"Why are you so late?" Her tone is stern and reaches the creases she's started getting on her forehead. For a moment she massages the bridge of her nose, eyes tightly shut before opening them again to look at me. "Go on. I'm waiting for a good excuse."

It's not that I don't have an excuse, but the one I do have won't be good enough for Mother. Still, pride wells up in my chest and this irrational urge to defend myself and what I do with my time overwhelms me. "I was reading to the boys. After all, you wanted me to volunteer my time and learn to give back. I take this very seriously."

My mother blinks at me, her perfectly coifed hair strikes me as strange for just a moment, so very unlike her.

"Well then," she says, and this time her voice is soft, with a tinge of resignation. "Next time I need you home in a timely manner, please don't read such a long tale."

She steps forward with a frown and wipes a finger along my fore-head. I'm surprised she doesn't try to shut my gaping mouth. Usually she'd point out how un-ladylike that is.

This time though she simply sighs. "You hurried, didn't you?"

I nod, a little taken aback by her sudden strange form of under-standing.

"Sweat is very unbecoming, Wendy. Go up, and I'll have some fresh water brought to your room." She moves away for a moment, and I gather my skirts to dash up the stairs, but her hand on my arm stays me suddenly.

"This is very important, Wendy. Not just for us, but for you and your future. I need you to understand that." She pauses, obviously waiting for some sort of reaction from me, so I nod tentatively.

Her face mellows and she pets my hand before letting go. "I'll come up and help you dress in a little while. Take your time washing up. You won't be able to lie down and rest, but you can at least be cool and collected."

Finally released from her strangely intense gaze and grasp, I head up the staircase, trying to ignore the uneasiness nagging at the back of my mind.

The stairs are simple, straight up and down. Nothing grandiose like the ones in the way-house. This place should feel homey, but even the faint smell of the apple tart cooling in the kitchen seems distant. Though Mother's hand is obvious in the precise placement of every-thing in the house, it feels impersonal, like we're on show. Then I remember, that at least for tonight, we are. The Davenports are important guests. Ambiguously so. Best behavior and all. There'll be no sneaking a boy to Neverland tonight.

Like the rest of the house, there's a slight chill to my room. When Joan knocks on the door to bring in a pitcher and fresh towels, my heart skips a beat. I know they're not telling me everything, and something tugs at the back of my consciousness. On the tip of my tongue and I can't quite get it out.

"Joan, is it fun to cook different things for dinner parties?"

She looks up at me a moment, one dark curl loose from her bun, and smiles. Her slight figure always reminds me of Tinkerbell, with a stubby nose, and delicate features. But her hands aren't as smooth, and her hair is dark.

And as soon as she speaks all similarity to a pixie vanishes. "Always, miss. I just love cookin'. Bit of a rush time though, wannit?"

Then they had only just cemented the visit. I grin back at her. "It certainly was last minute, but you cook some amazing food. I'm sure everything will be great." There. Mother always says to be charming, right?

A faint hint of color creeps into Joan's cheeks and she bows her head, avoiding my eyes. "Thanks, miss. You'd best wash-up."

She's finished and dashes out of the room before I can think of another question.

The water is warm and soft against my skin as I wash down my face and neckline, across my neck and chest. I wonder if Mother would really mind terribly if I just went to sleep and dreamt of places I'd rather be. I glance at my wardrobe and stop, still for a moment. Mother picked out my dress.

I've not seen it before. It's white with tiny pink flowers embroidered all the way down in mismatched lines so as to give the appearance of randomness. There's a tiny bolero-jacket trimmed with red velvet that goes over the shoulders. I reach a hand out tentatively to touch it, to make sure it's real, because surely something this fine, this ladylike—it can't be mine. I'm not even fifteen; I shouldn't be wearing things like this. Does my liking it mean I've already grown up?

"Do you like it?"

Mother's voice pitches low, and though she startled me slightly, I'm still wrapped up in the dress and everything it means.

"It looks pretty." A small smile tugs at her lips as she approaches me, and I should learn to think more before I speak, but the next words tumble out anyway. "How can I know if I like something before I put it on?"

Her expression doesn't change, and she picks it up, undoing the bolero carefully. I watch in rapt fascination as she pulls it off the hanger in preparation to help me don it. The dress is frightening. It represents everything I don't want. Adulthood, self-absorption, lies, and deception. But it's so pretty...

As we slip it over my head and tie the looser styled corset into place so it fits well, all I can do I stare in the mirror. With each layer of the dress, and finally the bolero, I can barely recognize myself. The material is fine and soft and amazing.

Mother smiles at me and hugs my shoulders, looking in the glass with me. "You look so beautiful, Wendy. Like the perfect young lady you will be."

It's all I can do to nod. Even I can see what she means staring back at us from the mirror. A stranger. An adult monster in training. And I know why she doesn't scream or hide, because my mother—all of the adults—they've already given over their childhoods.

~

The chandelier in the hall has been lit. We rarely do that, and it only makes me fear this dinner engagement more. Mother leads me into the dining room, which looks different than it did last night. There's a small standing area and the bench near the window has been uncluttered. Our dining table is fully extended and decked with the good silverware and dishes.

My father stands near the open windows, the drapes pulled neatly to the sides. His dark head is bowed as he speaks with Mr. Davenport next to him.

Mother walks me straight over to Father, and I notice that

standing in the corner are two more people. My stomach freezes over with dread. Father looks up as we approach and smiles briefly at my mother.

His gaze barely graces my form as he turns to the older man. "Mr. Davenport, you remember my daughter, Wendy."

Mr. Davenport extends a hand, and I take it in mine, studying the man just as he studies me. His black hair is smattered with generous amount of silver, even through to his mustache. Merry eyes twinkle at me as he smiles, and their shade of brown lights up his face. His hands are smooth, yet not soft as he withdraws them from my grasp.

"It's lovely to see you again, Wendy."

I blink at him and stammer a little when I respond. "Thank you, s-sir. Very much."

My father takes me by the elbow and whispers as he pulls me over to the far corner. "You've grown up so beautifully, Wendy."

I wish people would stop saying that. First Mrs. Davenport, my mother, her husband, and now my father. If that person behind Mrs. Davenport is who I think it is, I might just run and never come back.

"Here we go. No strangers to you. Chin up, you'll have to do all these sorts of engagements once you're married." He squeezes my elbow and moves me to stand in front of Mrs. Davenport and her son. Albert.

The cold in my stomach spreads up to my lungs, so that I don't realize I'm breathing in short gasps. For just a moment my vision clouds over and I remember the doll I got for my eighth birthday lying shattered at the foot of a tree because she couldn't fly. I remember Albert and his friends holding me at bay while they tried to see if a turtle's shell would break. And I clutch at the place on my arms where the bruises his fingers made seemed to take an eon to fade.

I've never wanted to run away to Neverland more.

"Wendy, you look absolutely beautiful!" Mrs. Davenport is gushing, but I can't rip my eyes away from Albert. That sneer I remember so well tugs at the right corner of his very fake smile. None of the expression reaches his dark eyes. The only twinkle in them is shady, dangerous, and cruel.

"You remember my son Albert, of course?" She smiles at me.

Mrs. Davenport is gorgeous. Her smile reaches her eyes and lights up her perfectly heart-shaped face. Blue eyes, much brighter than her older husband's, reflect the same joy at life, and as she takes my hand in both of hers, I'm quite certain this lady has never baked an apple tart in her life. She leads me to stand in front of him.

"You two used to play in the garden together as children, remember? Until a few years ago. You can talk about what you've been up to."

"Of course I remember Wendy." Albert stands up and takes my hand. Even now there's a slimy quality to it. I grit my teeth and force a smile.

"Hello, Albert." I'm not sure how I manage to grind it out evenly when my whole body is going into lock down. With his skin touching my own, I'm more afraid than Hook ever made me feel.

Albert's grip is strong and demanding and while his skin is smooth like his mother's, the strength in his fingers reflect his father. "I've been looking forward to seeing you again, Wendy." I can hear the hollowness to his words, but our mother's are beaming like the sun, blinding in their own ignorance. Even his smile seems radiant, but I know better. There's slime lingering underneath.

"I've been looking forward to seeing you again too," I lie glibly.

Perhaps if someone had actually mentioned that he'd be coming, I could have run away. Maybe they know? I peer at them and try to wrest my hand out of his grip. It's pinching me, crushing my fingers against each other. But he's still smiling, and our parents laugh and begin to walk away.

"You two have fun catching up on old times." I think that was Mrs. Davenport, but I'm too focused on not crying out in pain to notice. Finally, I snatch my hand out of his grip and glare at him.

"You haven't changed a bit." I bite out, as bold as I dare be with our parents so close. Albert is a chameleon and the best liar I've ever met.

He shrugs, and loses the smile, giving way to that smirk he wears so well.

"Oh," he says, looking me up and down so slowly that I need to fight off the heat I can feel rising in my cheeks. "But you have."

He finishes and stands, crossing his arms as if daring me to tell someone.

He always did that. I learned the hard way that no one would believe me over him.

"I'll be attending Cambridge in the fall." His words pull me back from my own frantic thoughts. Anything not to summon those memories again.

"Cambridge? I'm sorry. You're ready for university?" He's always seemed so juvenile, but I guess he is a few years my senior.

Albert nods. "It's my birthday this summer." He narrows his eyes, and a sinister air leaks through his next words. "Guess what I'm getting for my birthday."

My gut clenches, and I have to count each breath in and out to steady myself. All I do is shrug, because if I speak it might turn into a scream. He's so much older than I am. Almost three years.

He moves a little closer, and I freeze, not sure if he's going to whisper his gift into my ear, or bite me. But as if Joan can feel my discomfort, I'm saved by the dinner bell.

Mostly anyway. It appears my seat is next to Albert, distanced from all of our parents who chatter amongst themselves. My stomach ties in knots and my appetite flees in the face of what this might mean. How I wish I'd just walked that plank.

The sensation spreads in my stomach, all too familiar now. I want to run back to Neverland. Not for the first time I wish I'd stayed there all along. Safe with Peter, and the lost boys, needed and above all, understanding my place.

Mrs. Davenport leans over to me and pets my hand, breaking the spell. "Wendy, are you not hungry?"

I look up into those startling blue eyes, and for a moment they transfix me. It's long enough to gather my tattered dignity and thoughts before replying. I nod first, to buy another second.

"I'm well. It's been a long day." And I smile at her before turning my attention back to Albert.

I don't know if I can control myself enough not to blurt out that her son is a sadistic, lying, manipulator, and the last thing I need is to ruin my father's career for him.

"Mother said you volunteer?"

I cringe for a moment. Can they truly not hear the way he speaks? There's nothing kind or even human about it, but I can't cause a scene, not yet. Not while I'm so underprepared. So, I answer him. "Yes, at the local boy's shelter."

"What do you do?"

For a moment I want to show off, I want to tell him that I help little boys escape the people who force them to steal for them, who abuse their trust. I want to tell him that I can have him taken to Neverland and thrown to a crocodile. But I don't say any of that, because while I don't care what his opinion of me is, I care what his father thinks of mine. With any luck, I can just get through tonight and not have to see him for another three years.

So instead, I smile at him and fill it with as much niceness as possible. "I tell them faerie tales."

REVELATIONS

*U*p in my bedroom I can hear the Davenports saying goodbye to my parents. They all laugh in a cheerfully warming way, except the dull overtone of Albert's laugh. Such an empty sound. How his lovely parents produced such a son, I'll never understand.

I tug the bolero off and toss it to land in a heap on my bed, while I flick these horrible pointy shoes to nestle haphazardly against the curtains. My chest heaves, not only with the exertion but with the events of the evening. This dress is suffocating me, and I tug at the bindings in a fervor to escape it. Finally, I free enough of myself to push the bodice of the dress down. I thought it was beautiful when I first saw it, but now it's just a cocoon to change me into the adult I'm so desperate to avoid.

Laying on my bed with the dress half off, I look up at the ceiling. Crown molding hugs the edges, accenting the wallpaper Mother chose. Slowly, I glance at the wardrobe near the door, too far away from me right now. The window has a small table and chair in front of it. It's where I leave the candles to signal Peter that I have something for him. That I need him.

I wonder if I can light one now.

The door swings open, and I sit up hurriedly.

"Sorry, Mother," I say, ready to defend myself from whatever reason has brought her up here.

She surprises me by enveloping me in a hug and helps me free myself from the dress.

"You were amazing tonight, Wendy."

And even though I'm grateful for the compliment, it makes my stomach flutter with uneasiness. There's obviously something I don't understand.

"Thank you?" I venture, not wanting to sound like I don't appreciate her praise.

She surprises me again by laughing. "I wanted to see how you'd react to meeting Albert again."

It's an effort not to bite the words out. She's never seen the Albert I've seen, none of the adults have. "Why? They're family friends. I was polite."

"Oh, my love. You were excellent. I couldn't have asked for more." She touches my hand and looks at me for a moment.

Tension is building in my stomach, so much I think I might explode. Every word she's saying is weighted with something she's not telling me. Something to do with the Davenports. With Albert.

"You two used to have such a fun time playing together when you were younger."

I blink at her. Surely, she can't mean that? I always begged not to go, and the words are out before I can decide otherwise. "No, I didn't. Don't you remember how I hated visiting, how I wanted to stay home with Nanna?"

She pats my hand again, condescension leaking from her smile. "No little girls actually like playing with little boys. It's different now. You're grown up. He never let you out of his sight then, I'm sure it'll be even better now."

If I could back up I would, jump out the window and scream, but all that comes out is a whisper. "Please, Mother? Say it clearly."

My mother's shoulders sag briefly, but square away again before she looks at me directly. Her smile is a little grim and she breathes in deeply. She grabs my shoulders gently, but firmly, and pushes me to sit facing her on the bed before maneuvering herself too. "You moved out of the nursery a while ago now, Wendy."

"I know." Really? This isn't saying anything clearly.

"And to be honest, we might have let you stay in there a little longer than we should have for the sake of convenience, and a little for your brothers." This time I just nod while she looks at me because I don't trust myself to speak. "You're getting older. Old enough that you have to take on responsibilities and start performing adult tasks."

"That's why I come to volunteer with you, isn't it?" Panic starts to rise in my throat, the taste of bile sits at the back threatening to choke me because I know this isn't what she means. Denial beckons to me.

"Wendy, that's just one sort of preparation. Sweetheart, soon you need to be leaving this nest, starting a family and making your own way, your own place in this world. We need to make sure you're taken care of."

"What? Leave here? Have my own children? I'm not even fifteen!" My hands are shaking even more than my voice, and my mother grips them gently in hers.

"Sweetie, you're fifteen in a month. It's a lot to take in now, but this is just how things need to be."

"What? Now? When?" My thoughts are swirling and I can't grab any of them for long enough to compile into coherent thoughts, into an argument my mother might think valid.

"Well, not right now." She laughs as if it's the funniest thing in the world. "You two need time to catch up, to see the beautiful adults you've both become."

"Albert will never be beautiful." I mutter the words out loud before I can reign myself in, but I don't regret it.

Not even when mother frowns and squeezes my hands a little too hard. "Now Wendy. Don't be childish. We've spent a long time setting this up. You should appreciate that you'll have a husband who can look after you."

I blink at her words as they sink to the bottom of my stomach and stay there. Husband?

I guess I know what Albert's birthday present is now.

~

I don't hear another word Mother says. Not in her defense nor in Father's. Not one justification. Not another lie. I simply remove my slip and slide into my nightgown, pushing past her to make it to my bed, to get her out of my room. The one thing I can pretend is mine, this domain they gave me. Even if it's contingent on doing what they ask.

I shouldn't be surprised. Albert is the perfect solution in their eyes, the one to take care of their troubled daughter. I'm quite aware that I've always been stubborn and opposed to some of the things they do, but that they won't even listen to me? My own parents? No wonder the boys at Stepney have such horrid chances of anyone believing them.

Mother leaves eventually. Pity sleep doesn't come and pay me a visit. The crown molding looks down at me in the lamplight, both of them mocking me with their age and service to humankind. I wish I'd never come back from Neverland.

Neverland.

I sit up in bed, wondering if it's all right for me to see Peter, to glimpse Neverland. I've only had occasion to help two boys cross over after Tinkerbell visited me a few months ago about the tea. She showed me where to get the plant and how to crush the berries so it would help magnify the pixie dust. But I've always been hesitant to drink it. Because it means admitting I don't have a place here anymore, admitting Neverland is my only option.

But that doesn't mean I can't take a peek, does it? I'm sure I can look for the stars, keep my eyes peeled for Peter's shadows and hope that maybe, just maybe I'll see them flitting about out there. After all, it was on just such a night that I first met them.

I move quietly, sure that some time has passed since Mother left, since the Davenports left. My parents are probably asleep already.

Sound asleep, safe in their machinations' success and my relegation as just another piece of chattel.

There are women in London fighting for the right to vote! To vote! How can we be viewed as so much less than men when we're not? Are we? Didn't I prove that in Neverland? At least to myself. If I have to grow up, I want to go to London and fight for our rights and be the voice of children no one listens to. They don't even know the real Albert, but I've seen it; I've experienced it. Mother always dismissed it as another of my tales.

Now my stomach is roiling, and the anger sets in as I tug my nightshirt off and dive around in my closet for a plain navy blue smock. Mother didn't think I kept any, but I did. So much more comfortable than the things she makes me wear now. I can handle less fashionable if it means I might get a chance to see the star.

But as I go to creep down the stairs, I'm surprised by the light still on in the dining room. I creep slowly, avoiding the sixth step from the bottom because it squeaks without fail every time someone puts weight on it. Crouching on the last step, I sit and listen. I have a good track record with eavesdropping.

Father sounds so different. His voice is tired, deeper. "Are we doing the right thing?"

I expect mother to reply adamantly, immediately, but I'm surprised by the long pause before she does so. "This secures her a future, one where she'll always be comfortable and never want for anything."

"And we become a part of the family business, too."

I choke down a gasp at my father's derisive tone. He doesn't sound happy, and he should. Shouldn't he? Isn't he about to get his dream career path if he marries me off to Albert?

There's a rustling of fabrics against each other and finally, I hear my mother speak. Her tone is softer, sadder than I think I've ever heard her before, and now I understand why people shouldn't eavesdrop. Not everything is way-houses and rainbows.

"Remember when we found out we would have Wendy?"

There's no answer, so I can only hope Father nods because if he forgot that, I'll think less of him.

"And we knew it would be expensive, and we worked at that budget and saved and slaved. Just like we have with every child since then. We always said we had to be able to afford our children."

"I know. I know."

But Mother pushes on. At least she's not only that way with me. "We've always agreed to provide the utmost best for our children. And Wendy needs solid surroundings, a household to manage so she doesn't focus on those daydreams."

"And her daydreams get so vivid." My father's plaintive sigh echoes out into the foyer.

"You're giving her what we can't. What, no matter how hard we try, we'll never be able to afford for her." Now my mother speaks with conviction, and while I understand her logic, I find many faults in it.

"Does she even like Albert?" I can feel his resolve quavering and will him not to give in. Just one of them, I just need one of them on my side.

There's another rustle that I can't quite define before mother speaks, some of that conviction gone. "She knows him. They've known each other for years. And he was malleable to the idea, despite the stories she's spun."

I think I hear him put his head in his hands, and it's a few moments before he speaks again. "I remember talking about it so many years ago, and now my little girl is grown up. Shouldn't we give her a choice? What if she doesn't like him?"

My mother laughs. "She's hesitant now, but they're not betrothed yet. It's a long way off. She has time to get used to marriage."

"But does she want to?"

My father sums it up perfectly. If only he knew.

"Love can be learned. She's barely an adult. She doesn't know what she wants yet, nor does she understand what she might need."

Father chuckles and his shadow moves, stands up to stretch. "Do any of us ever know?"

I start moving as soon as he does. Since the way out the front is blocked, I make my way up through to the attic and look at the stars. I can't see the second star from my room and right now, I need to think.

So many emotions battle in my head. Indignation is the loudest, desperation a close second.

The attic stairs are hidden behind what looks like a closet door. They're rickety and we're constantly warned to stay away from them, but just like the main staircase, they're fine if you know where to step. There's only one window in the attic and it's away from the piles that seem to grow after every Christmas, away from the sheet-covered furniture we never used from our previous house.

The window is huge, and for this part of London, it's a lovely view. Over the nursery, and straight in line with the second star on the right. Maybe if I watch it for long enough, I'll find a way to it without Peter, without Tink, and I can just get lost in Neverland forever.

I know what I don't want. This forcible growing up. This constant barrage of disappointment in what becoming an adult seems to mean. A lessening of myself, decisions that will never be my own, with my visits to the way-house the only deviation from my scheduled life.

I just want to go and see Peter. He made everything else seem trivial, and everyone else so inconsequential. His smile, his eyes, even his funny little green outfit. I want him to be the one sitting next to me at the dinner table. How do I get away from Albert?

And worse, how will I tell Thomas my parents have picked a husband?

DAWN

Sleep is elusive, and the star shines so brightly I think it's beckoning me. For a few moments, I'm moving toward it, wind underneath me, ruffling my hair, breath in short gasps. But I blink and everything vanishes, snapping me back where I stand behind the safety of the window bars. Slowly the night sky begins to lighten, and I shake myself out of my partial doze. If I don't get down to my room and leave before Mother checks in on me, I'll have to wait for her and walk the way to the Causeway with her. I'm still unsure of how to address this whole Albert fiasco. There's still this part of me that's huddling in a corner in disbelief.

The real reason I returned from Neverland was that taking all three of us from my parents at once seemed unusually cruel. Right now, they'll only lose me, if I can find a way to follow the Stepney boys. I push through the door from the attic only to find Michael sucking on his thumb, trailing teddy with the other hand, looking directly at me.

"Michael, what is it?"

Something must be wrong with him or John. Please not John. I struggle to breathe as panic grips my chest.

"You don't look sick," I say, trying to keep my voice steady as I feel for his temperature, and check his pulse.

He shakes his head, soft waves of hair bouncing in a way some women pay a fortune for at the salon.

"Was looking for you. Bed was empty." His big eyes well with tears, and I pull him into a hug. It's still mostly dark in the hall, with only the light from the window at the end of it illuminating anything at all. He clings to me, tiny hands weaving into my smock as I pick him up and carry him to my bedroom. John probably slept through him leaving and everything. Boy could always sleep like...well, whatever it is that sleeps really well. The dead?

By the time I reach my bed, Michael is already asleep. It's easy to loosen his grip ever so slightly and lay him down, his head resting on my pillow. He looks so peaceful; his little stub nose catches a stray beam of light through the curtains of my window. Maybe he'll dream of futures that don't involve an Albert. Maybe I can live through his dreams. I leave him lying on the bed, teddy clutched to his side, mouth a little slack where a line of drool is starting to form.

My choice of dress today is easy. Blue and black stripes, it's as close to the types of smocks I wore before I moved out of the nursery as Mother let me possess. If I have to go about this endless routine, then at least I'll wear something comforting. The matching hat is far too big for my head, and I tug it over my hair after brushing hurriedly. Michael will be fine in my bed. At least he's home, and he's a boy— there is far less unknown out there for him.

The house is still silent as the first true rays of morning break through the windows. I wish we had stained glass somewhere, I should think I'd spend hours distracting myself with it. I choose a parasol and handbag before kissing Michael lightly on the forehead and dashing downstairs, skipping that sixth step with practiced ease.

Joan is surprised to see me as I dance around the corner, through the kitchen door she's just about to come in through.

"Morning to you," I say, forcing a smile onto my face. "I'll take these off your hands. I'm headed that way."

And I grab the large paper bag of rolls for the Causeway that Joan brings with her every morning.

If I'm going to be early, I may as well appear like I planned the whole thing. My head keeps rehashing the previous evening and wanting to dwell on things I can't currently change. What I need is a plan, and not the one that it's taking me all my willpower to resist. Neverland isn't the answer yet, not while the boys need me. And I know they do. I've seen those bruises, the fear in their eyes, and the way they occasionally cringe when someone enters the teaching room.

Since they don't have a big sister, they need a Peter Pan. I have too many things I need to take care of first, so I can't just run away. I'd do the same for my brothers, and I want them to be proud of a brave and resolute sister, not the coward who fled. I'll figure out the Albert situation.

I rarely come to the orphanage by myself. What is imposing and monstrous to me when my mother is by my side becomes daunting and nightmarish when I'm alone. I stop outside the door we usually take, knowing full well I'm a couple of hours early today. I'd just wanted something to focus on, and there was nothing else I could think of to do.

Mustering all the courage I possess, I march up the steps, hoping there's purpose to my stride. Mrs. Johnson, in her no-nonsense black ensemble, raises an eyebrow as I stride into the kitchen.

"Early today, love?" she asks even though it's very apparent that I'm there.

"Woke up early. Thought I'd get a head start." For a moment I stand there, not entirely certain what it is I should do, before I remember the hulking brown bag in my arms and hand it to her.

"Good then. We can always use an extra hand or three in the morning. Can you butter up some bread?"

Glad to have something to do, I nod and don one of the aprons hanging on a hook. The bread is thick and warm, fresh out of the oven. It smells so good that my stomach rumbles, and I recall I forgot to have any breakfast in my mad dash out of the house.

"Woke up so early ye forgot to eat I'm guessing?" Mrs. Johnson's smile reaches her eyes. It's nothing like Mrs. Davenport's though. It's sweet and genuine.

"Perhaps not the best of plans." I admit. Even though I know she's busy, even though I know she doesn't even have time to listen to the boys' plights, a hunk of warm, buttered bread is thrust into my hand.

"Eat up. Can't have you dying of hunger and working with food now, can we?" Her expression returns to the one marred by worry lines and wrinkles, but for a moment she gives me a glimmer of hope that not all adults have to turn out badly.

And then I remember that not listening is just as bad as lying, and the bread suddenly threatens to choke me.

~

*R*aucous talking echoes through to me from the dining area. It's the first time I've been here this early, and they all seem so happy to be alive. Despite everything, they make the most of it.

"Wendy!" Tybalt grabs my hand, pumping my arm up and down as if I were a water well. His fingers are thin but strong, and the bruising is fading around his neck. I barely resist the urge to hug him tightly. He's not my brother. It wouldn't be proper.

"Settle down." I try to sound stern but fail abysmally.

His happy face and exuberant charm win me over every time. I can't imagine Tybalt ever having to do what someone else says. It's probably part of the reason they honed in on him as one of their gets. I'm willing to bet that pick-pocketing and whatever else he has to do is easier for him personality-wise, but I think his conscience suffers. His slender frame makes him appear more fragile than he is, but I still don't want to chance another round of beatings or the solitary room in the basement. So near the river here, the damp can't be good for their lungs.

The hand that rests on my shoulder sends a chill down my spine. Spinning around, I fear the worst. Albert knows where I volunteer.

But instead of him, it's my mother, her brows knit together with what might be concern. "Joan said you brought the bread over early."

"I was awake." My answer is so quick, I can see Mother processing it thoughtfully. At least that's something. She tugs at my elbow and pulls me back into the kitchen, into a corner nowhere near anyone else. "Wendy, I need to ask you something very sensitive."

My stomach ties itself in knots and then gradually starts to work itself out. Maybe she's realized I wasn't lying about Albert, that he truly is monstrous. Maybe she'll listen if I tell her the things he really did when he was a child and that I'm scared of what he'll do as an adult.

"There was a young boy here, by the name of David. Did you know him?"

I wasn't expecting her to say that. My heart sits in my throat as all thoughts of Albert wash away and I fight not to replace it with pure panic. I shrug slowly to buy time while my brain races for an appropriate answer. "I knew him from the lessons, about as well as I know any of them."

Apparently, it was the right thing to say if Mother's sigh is any indication. "I thought so, but I just wanted to caution you. It seems he's run off. So just—Wendy, be careful, please?"

Normally, I would think she's being sweet. Mother does have moments of warmth, but the request now doesn't instill me with confidence in her. I smile, because she expects it and right now I can't afford for her to watch me more than usual.

"Of course, Mother. I'm always careful."

She squeezes my shoulders, and either she's unaware of how I feel about last night, of the stiffness in my attitude toward her, or she's just determined to ignore it. I turn away from her, heading toward the common area to give the boys one of their stories.

Two men stand in the room. Tybalt and another—I think the other boy is Stephen—stand next to them. Their hands rest on the boys' shoulders, and both youth's faces are pinched and pale. I've never seen the men before, but they have the same garb on that some of the handy-workers around the orphanage have, and instinctually I know who they are.

White hot anger flashes behind my eyes, and I want to scream at them, to yell, to feed them to crocodiles. Instead, I clap my hands, startling the men and catching the boys' attention.

"Story time, boys." Sometimes I show them the letters I know and try to teach them to read as well, but today I think I need to tell them a tale even more than they need to hear it.

I watch them, as they gather in front of me, their faces all flushed again, so much hope in their eyes. Every one of us knows David is in a safer place now. Each of the boys in this room dread that one will be called to replace him, because that's how it works. Maybe we should just burn the building to the ground and let Peter take them all.

"Wendy?" One of the younger boys, a little older than Michael approaches me hesitantly. He's cute and chubby and probably won't remember any of my stories in a few years. I wonder if Michael already thinks Neverland is just a story I tell. The thought tears at my heart a little and I file it away for later contemplation.

"Yes, Joshua?" I kneel down to his eye level and hold his pudgy hands.

He flinches slightly, and it's then I notice the slight rings around his wrists and finger indents, like he's been grabbed roughly. For a moment my temper wells up and threatens to blind me, but his hesitant question snaps me back. "Can you tell us the tale about Captain Hook and the crocodile?"

I bite down on the revulsion in my throat. The comparison of Albert to Hook last night was far too close for comfort, but for these little guys, if that's really what they want to hear, then I'll oblige them. "You want to hear how Captain Hook lost his hand to the big old Croc?"

A cheer goes up from the gathering in front of me, and the smile spreading across my face is real and warm. These children lift my spirits up. Maybe I can preserve this instance for them, this happiness, and these dreams at this age by taking them to Neverland. Nothing will change for them there. Only memories of home will fade while new ones take over during the passing through to the lost boys' cove.

If anyone deserves Neverland, it's these boys. But I have so much to do. The stories here, figuring out how to put a stop to this arrangement my parents have made with the Davenports. Expectant faces look at me with hope ingrained in their smiles. What I need to concentrate on is right now.

"Right, then," I say. "Hook it is."

And I tell them about their Neverland.

REQUEST

The boys never fail to enjoy Hook's plight. Maybe it's an adult getting his comeuppance for trying to control the children. Maybe it's the way the tick-tock of the crocodile's constant presence is a stark warning of how his time is running out.

It's the closest I've come to understanding what it means to get older. Time moves faster, because you've been alive longer, and it's always out of reach. Father never seems to have enough of it, and Mother always has a schedule. Being an adult means prioritizing what you can fit into your days and be damned how honest or observant a life you lead.

The movement of Mother's hand as she waves to me from the dining hall door interrupts the dark thoughts swirling in my head. I raise a hand to answer her gesture, knowing I'll have to leave as soon as this story is done. She smiles, and the tension seeps from her shoulders, like she wasn't sure if I'd acknowledge her. There are lines around her mouth and eyes I swear weren't there yesterday afternoon, and my stomach knots itself for a moment while I think it might be because of me. I watch her leave and notice the queasiness doesn't really abate because when it all comes together I feel a bit sorry for Mother.

"So, Wendy? Does he ever catch the croc?" Tybalt interrupts my thoughts this time, with that sunshiny smile I wish John wore more often. Maybe you have to experience hardships to truly appreciate other things.

"He's still chasing him," I say as I lean forward, clutching the book to my chest.

"Still?" Joshua's eyes are always big, but right now they seem the size of saucers holding a hot drink of chocolate, decadent and eerie. He's slight of build with wild black hair that never seems to be tamed.

"Still." I answer, trying to sound formidable while I inspect Joshua as well as I can for signs that he too has been recruited for the thieving ring.

"But you don't know now, do you?" Marcus crosses his arms and fixes me with a stare. The light lilt to his voice always catches me off guard and I'm never quite certain if he means the condescension or not.

"Not right now. He might be asleep," I say, straightening back up and watching my words carefully.

I'm not entirely sure how many of them believe me, and Marcus is one of the older boys. We don't need the adults stopping us before we can save more of the younger ones.

Marcus grins triumphantly and nods. "Thought so."

"Well, except the croc never sleeps." I wink at the boys, and grin. "After all, the tick-tock playing deep in his belly keeps him up most of the night. It's part of the reason he chases Hook so. Driven mad and hungry because he can't sneak up on his food anymore. Maybe one day, he'll find someone to replace the old man!"

The boys sit back and gasp, eyes wide with what I hope is mock horror. I suppress the smile I can feel tugging at my lips and turn to the hand that grazes my elbow ready to answer another question. My breath hitches in my throat as I look at a plaid-covered chest. It's not one of the little boys; it's Thomas. I have to look up a little, angling my neck to see those merry green eyes.

Funny how they're not full of dark secrets like Peter's. Thomas's eyes are as open and honest as he is.

"These youngins troubling you, miss?" he asks with mock politeness, tipping an imaginary hat in my direction.

"No, sir. They're just questioning Neverland and the powerful ticktock croc." I smile at him.

Even though he wasn't there, even though he's never seen it, Neverland binds us. A few months ago he asked if it was real, because of how I spoke of it with such reverence. It took several more hasslings from him and some of the younger boys, but now they know, and now he has a way to save those going through the ringer.

Thomas laughs and his whole face lights up. He's never been overly good at staying in character. "Did you make it in time?"

His question takes me by surprise and I have to check myself to make sure I've understood.

"Last night..." And the whole debacle comes back to me. Can I even tell Thomas? Would he understand? Will he regard me differently or as less? Might he spend less time with me, talking to me? I can't handle any of that. "Last night went fine. Father had guests."

I put all my effort into making a funny grimacing face and it works, because he laughs with me instead of showing concern. All the while my heart beats fast and I feel a little flushed, a bit scared.

He's watching me, a strange look I've not seen before on his face where his eyebrows tweak down a little, and his nose is slightly scrunched.

"Are you okay?" I ask belatedly, remembering my manners. I'm still in denial and while I could use help figuring out what to do, I'm not ready to go down that train of thought yet. Does he already know?

Thomas nods, and draws in a deep breath. "Wendy, I have a big favor to ask of you."

"Ask away. I can only say no." I manage to be so much bolder when talking to him than when talking to anyone else.

If I could be like this with my parents, I wouldn't be in this Albert mess. It's part of the reason I love to talk to Thomas. He brings out a side of me I have to be careful with everywhere else.

"With David gone too now, they're reaching to some of the

younger, smaller boys." He looks at me briefly and bites his lip, before focusing his gaze on the other side of the room instead.

I know it's hard for him to speak about this. He knows it so well because he went through it. Resisting the urge to hug him and stroke his hair and tell him everything will turn out for the best is one of the hardest things I've done. Right up there with leaving Neverland. But I also know that he needs to help these boys, so he can work through and make sense of things himself. I only wish I could do more.

"Who, Thomas?" I say the words softly, because he's stuck in memories he can't share with me, I can see it in the distance in his eyes. I push a little more, because I want him to know that at least *I* notice. "Other than Tybalt, who else?"

His eyes meet mine briefly before he looks away again and breathes out the names. "Joshua, Henry, and Stephen."

I gasp a little. "Three at once?"

"We took two from them, Wendy. They need more. It's like they're gearing up in case someone else runs away from them." He runs a hand through his already disheveled hair, before finally focusing on me. "Are we doing the right thing?"

It's a question I wish I had an answer for, but I don't know myself. "Should we do nothing? Isn't doing nothing worse than ignoring the fact that something bad is happening?" I hope he can answer that, because it's a question I've been asking myself for months now.

Thomas shrugs and sighs, almost like he's about to give up. "We can't just stand by and watch this happen if we can help. We can't."

The knots of tension in my shoulders relax a little. "Maybe, if we get enough of them away from here, we can start mentioning things they've said before they ran?"

Thomas perks up a little, his eyes bright. "You mean, drop hints that they were scared of downstairs, of the things they were asked to do?"

I nod, because I can't abandon these boys. They're here with me every day, cheering me up, giving me something that I feel good about. I help them find escapism, help them learn. I'll make sure the way-house never sells if I have to. The only obstacle is Peter, but these boys are young enough, I'm sure he'll take them. There'll just be more members to join in the Lost Boys' fun.

"Wait, though. There is one thing." I frown for a moment and look up at him.

"It's all right, Wendy." The tone in Thomas's voice changes from hopeful to destitute just in those few words and I feel awful for having been so vague just now.

"No, no. It's nothing bad." I stand up a little straighter, until I'm almost at eye level. "Just, Tybalt is one of them. We have to help him too.

"It's not bad?" his brow pinches a little. I've confused him.

Thomas looks away, biting his lip, eyes on the doorway to the dining hall. I know he's particularly close with Tybalt, like brothers. He probably doesn't want him to leave. Chatter and laughter filters through to us, and his expression changes until a small but warm smile lingers on his lips. I've never seen Peter look like that. For as much as Thomas can resemble him, there's a world of difference between the two, and Thomas never makes me feel like I'm inferior.

"He can't keep going through that, can he? He's not strong enough."

"But Neverland is so far away, Wendy." Thomas won't look at me.

I form my words carefully, to hit home what it is we're doing in saving these boys, in never letting them grow up. "It's forever away. It's never coming back away. But you've known that from the start."

For a few moments it seems Thomas won't let me in, he's putting up walls. His eyes cloud over a little and he refuses to meet my gaze. But just when I'm about to give up, his shoulders sag and he finally speaks.

"Not all the boys are as lucky as I was. I'm tougher, more resilient." He falls silent for a moment, and I need to let him know.

"My mother asked me about David."

"She what?" he says, whipping his head down a bit to look at me. Panic dances on the edges of his pupils as he waits for my answer.

"Mother asked me if I knew David. I told her not better or worse than I know anyone else here." This time I sigh. I don't like that I'm deceiving people, but we wouldn't have to if they'd actually listen to the boys making the complaints. But no one does, not even the chaplain who counsels the students for Sunday school.

"We're orphans. Adults expect us to run away." Thomas pinches the bridge of his nose with his finger and thumb. The scowl consumes his face in a way I've never seen before. It'd be fascinating if there wasn't such a bitterness to the words, such truth.

For a brief moment, I rest hand on his arm, trying to convey some measure of comfort through the touch. His skin is softer than I'd expect. The scowl lessens, and he smiles at me.

Squaring my jaw, I give him my own smile. "So we'll send them to Neverland."

"I think Neverland is the only place for them. They'll end up together, won't they?" His eyes beseech me, bleeding that warm green into everything he says.

"They'll end up together. No one but the other lost boys, and Peter..."

Thomas smiles. "Will they run into Hook? Have adventures?"

The latter makes me laugh, because of everything I remember most, even though I was scared at the time, the Hook encounter glows in my memory. A beacon of the things I am capable of, of the strong person I can be. "All the adventure."

"Can't we all go?" He asks, moving a little closer, bowing his head and refusing to meet my eyes and I can't help the hesitation that grips a hold of my tongue when my initial instinct is to say yes. Thomas is so close to me now, more than just my hand is touching his arm. My skirts brush against his trousers, and my breath hitches just a little. If only we could stand this way forever, he lends me such strength.

But I shake my head. "If we all go, who would be here to watch out for the rest?"

Thomas's shoulders slump and he sighs softly. "They'll be safe though, won't they?"

"They'll be children forever."

"Forever?" he whispers to me.

I sigh because it's such a long time, but square my shoulders and speak firmly. "Forever."

Forever didn't daunt Thomas at all in the way it should, and I'm not sure why it gives me such hesitation. After all, isn't this a good thing?

"There's so much to plan, so much to think about." His eyes light up and I'm suddenly a little wary.

"I can't take you with me, Thomas." I stress the words, trying to make them heavy and force him to understand.

He sighs. "You're afraid I'll try to sneak along?" It's said teasingly, a slight wink at the end of it, but for a few moments I really have to think about my motivations, or lack thereof, in taking him with me.

I have to clear my head, so I take a step back away from the headiness our proximity gives me. I remember David, calming down so peacefully, waiting to meet Peter. I remember James, lying on the cushions when I came to get him after dinner, smiling so happily as he met the Peter I'd told them so much about. Maybe I don't want him to meet Peter, maybe I don't want Thomas to never grow up if it means doing so without me.

"Yeah," I reply, forcing my own smile to the fore. "Something like that."

VISIT

$\mathcal{E}$ven though the reasons the boys need Neverland are nefarious, I can't help the excitement I feel dancing a jig through my body. It'll be a challenge to get them out, to avoid the watch. I'll have to take different routes home, of course. Can't have the watch or the lamplighters getting used to my face, especially if I travel with different boys each time.

I've always enjoyed making lists, and marking this one off as I walk home makes the journey pass by in a flash. Our gate is suddenly in front of me and I blink a few times at the glint of the sun off the windows, orientating myself for a few moments. Watch patrols. Lamplighter routine. Scout out different routes. Check. Need to get all of that done.

Opening the gate, I lift my skirts as I walk up the steps, suddenly in a grand mood. Things will be so much better for the boys where they're safe and together. And my life will have purpose for having helped them. That I get glimpses into the Neverland I miss so much? That's just a bonus. Our plans will work, they have to. The boys depend on us. I am strong, I can do this.

So regardless what else I have going on in my life, I can't afford to let it distract me from them. Although, sooner or later, I'll probably have to deal with this Albert situation.

I dust my skirts off and reach for the doorknob only to have it open in front of me. It takes me a few moments to adjust to the dimness in the hall, but I let out a short gasp before I can contain it. Albert stands in front of me with his beautiful smile. For just a moment it appears as if he's genuine, and then it's like there's a darkness shrouding him, enveloping us both, but it might just be a trick of the sun. All I want to do is turn tail and run to the way-house, and find a way out of here.

But he reaches forward and grabs my hand, tugging me sharply into the house. His fingers don't relinquish their hold as Mother approaches us, and they dig into my skin, causing me to bite my lip at the discomfort.

"Albert! You're a guest, you didn't need to open the door." She smiles in the coquettishly fake way that makes me feel ill.

And Albert? Returns the expression a million times more slyly. He reminds me of the Cheshire cat in that Wonderland tale. Wonderland is not to be confused with Neverland. I don't think I'm a Wonderland sort of girl.

"Mrs. Darling. I saw Wendy approaching through the window and just had to open the door for her." His grip sears through my skin. I'll check for singe marks if he ever lets go.

"You're such a sweet boy, Albert." She pats him on the shoulder, apparently oblivious to his hand crushing my own, and the tears welling my eyes. "Now come along you two, let us have tea in the den. We even have some of those shortbread biscuits you love so much, Wendy."

If I open my mouth, it'll be to scream, so I just nod and hope she sees it. I refuse to give into this game he's playing and give him the satisfaction of causing me pain.

"Don't you two look lovely together?" Mrs. Davenport coos as we walk into the room. Her hair is arranged in this majestically complex set of twists and turns, so much that I feel drab in my dress and suddenly conspicuous hat. Still, I wonder what our mothers are drinking in their tea. After all, I'm quite certain my face isn't a reflection of any type of happiness.

My mother doesn't seem to care. "Aren't they just adorable?"

The women share a laugh, and I feel about to pass out. I don't think he's breaking my fingers, but if they're not bruised, I'll be extremely surprised.

It's Mrs. Davenport who provides me some release. "Now, Wendy. You just come and sit next to me and I'll help you unpin that lovely hat of yours." She pats the seat next to her and Albert finally releases my hand. The pain as blood rushes back into my fingers and the pressure releases has tiny black spots dancing in front of my eyes. I think I may have inadvertently let out a small cry, because as I almost fall into the seat beside his mother, the corners of her mouth tilt down and her brow furrows.

"Wendy, dear? Are you all right?" she asks as she pets my arm, the one with the good hand. "Are you not feeling well?"

She reaches for my forehead, but I've had enough of being touched by Davenports for one day and I shy back a bit but try to mollify her with a smile.

"I'm a little tired. It was a busy morning in the kitchen, and the boys do love their stories." Her hand withdraws and the frown is turned upside down.

"Here," she says gently, "Let me help you with that hat."

I turn a little in the seat, nursing my hand against my lap. I'm sure I can see a few bruises already forming on the back of it. He really does have a strong grip. This burst of sensation sweeps through me. From my feet through to my head, a flutter of chill winding its way up my spine. I think I'm even more scared of growing up because of him. But right now, at least our mothers are here. He wouldn't do anything worse than this hand squeezing thing with them here, would he?

"And have you given a thought to any of the societies you might like to patron, Wendy?" Mrs. Davenport's question intrudes on my thoughts and draws me back to the present.

"Societies?" I say, tasting the word on my tongue for good measure and trying to wrack my brains to think what she means.

Mother is in a few. Patron of the arts, although she's only just joined that one. I think she's been a ballet patron for much longer and that's definitely the one I prefer. Such pretty dancing, and all of it for the love.

"Ballet," I reply, hoping I didn't misread the question.

"Just ballet?" Mrs. Davenport's eyes sparkle like I imagine the ocean does. She's teasing me and ruffles my hair in such a childlike manner I'd be offended if I cared enough.

"She is just getting started now," My mother reminds with a light and chipper tone. Strange how much she changes when other people are near. "Before too long I'll take her to a few meetings and let her see for herself how they work."

"Oh, excellent idea!" Mrs. Davenport claps her hands softly before reaching for her cup of tea off to the side. "Perhaps I will have the chance to do so too. If you'd like to come with me, that is, Wendy."

I nod, because I genuinely like this woman. Albert says nothing. All he does is sit in his chair, sipping a cup of tea and watching me. His smile is soft, but I know what it truly hides. His gaze never wavers, his eyes never express anything except that bottomless darkness that seemed to want to suck my soul. In a morbid sort of way, he's fascinating, trying to draw me in, to drown me and control me. Several times I catch myself on the precipice about to fall in. He's really nothing like his parents.

Is he a changeling? I read once that those faerie tale creatures are evil and meant to deceive humans and their offspring. But he doesn't seem faerie-like. Because I'm such an expert, of course.

Neverland had darkness. And for just a moment, a blink of my eyes, he sits there on that pirate ship instead of Hook, has me bound and about to walk the plank. Except there would be no Peter to save me, because there is more bad in Albert than there ever was in Hook. The room floods in again from the edges, and finally leaves him sitting in that high backed chair again, outlined against the velvet drapes behind him. He sits on it like a throne.

I sigh and look away from him, unaware of just how long I'd been observing him in the same way he watched me.

"Oh look," Mrs Davenport laughs. Even that noise is pretty coming from her. "We must be boring the children."

My mother's laugh isn't as pretty, but it's sweet, and I wish it were real instead of to impress. She glances at the grandmother clock hanging on the other side of the room. "It is getting late. And I do know you have dinner plans.".

Mrs Davenport follows her gaze and gasps. "Oh, yes. I didn't realize the time had got away from us so much. But before we go. Albert, when did you say you wanted to take Wendy on an outing?"

This time I gasp, and from the secretive smiles our mothers give each other, I think they assume I'm smitten. How do I stop them from thinking that? I don't understand why this is all happening so quickly, and my stomach twists and turns. But even while I flounder to try and figure it out, Albert is offering them his ingratiating smile. Like he did when we were children, except an adult, more sophisticated version of it. He's all grown up, and he wants to drag me down with him.

"On a weekend. Perhaps? I'm not sure yet. I still have to make arrangements, and I'd really like it to be a bit of a surprise, if that's acceptable of course?" He phrases it like he's truly excited, but I know better. It's just like when we went to visit, how he'd grab my hand and tug me away feigning excitement and interest at playing together.

"You are welcome to step out anytime, Albert." My mother's tone infuriates me.

"Except when I'm at the orphanage," I pipe up. "I've committed to them, and the boys have come to look forward to their stories and lessons."

I make sure to keep my tone strong and even. It was the first thing that popped into my head, my only defense.

My mother blinks, Mrs. Davenport smiles, and while their eyes are averted, Albert's smile sears into me. If I look long enough, I'm sure I'll see it crack.

"Of course! It's an admirable thing to keep one's commitments." Mrs Davenport takes my hands in hers before standing up and pulling me with her. Even that light touch sends pain shooting through my slowly bruising hand, and I fight the grimace I can feel approaching. She pulls me into a brief hug, and holds me at arm's length again. "I'm so glad you've grown into the lovely young lady we always hoped you would."

This time I blink. "Thank you, Mrs. Davenport." I can't detect any type of duplicity in what she says. It's like she truly wants what's best for her son. It's like she doesn't know him.

Mother and I escort them into the foyer and bid them farewell.

"I'll see you soon, Wendy," Albert says as his goodbye, and the threat of it sends shivers down my spine.

~

The moment the door closes, my mother rounds on me.

"How could you be so rude!"

I take a step back, unsure of what I did. All the while they were here I tried to think of a way to get out of this, I was as polite as I could be.

"What do you mean? I was politer than I've ever been!"

"He's your intended. Or he will be if you don't chase him away, and you can't chase him away. How could you be so demanding? *Not when you're volunteering?*" She steps toward me and the bannister stands in my way of fleeing. "If you keep this up, there will be no more volunteering!"

I can feel the heat prick the back of my eyes, and will the tears to stay at bay.

"I won't let you take that away from me." My voice is steadier than I anticipated, and suddenly the pit in my stomach turns to stone, one to lean on, not a heavy one. "Do you not see what he's like? Do you want to be rid of me that much?"

I don't raise my voice, because that's counterproductive. I remain cool and collected, because I genuinely want to know.

My mother steps back this time, a frown on her face. "Stop making things up, Wendy. You *always* make things up."

"My stories?" I ask, raising an eyebrow. "Most stories are made up,

Mother. Including the one where you think he didn't torment me as a child."

"Oh, Wendy." She waves her hand dismissively, but there's a heaviness to the action, like she's tired. "All little boys torment little girls. It's how they show their affection."

"What?" She can't seriously be thinking of the word torment in the same way I am. "And what when they torment young ladies?"

My volume has dropped so low it's almost a whisper, but it echoes through the foyer as the wind whips it around. I hold out my hand, the bruising I knew would be there is coming to the fore, dark and purple, and ugly.

Mother's lips part ever so slightly and she pinches her nose for a moment. I'm happy I've shocked her. But her words are not what I expect. "He might be pushing boundaries, but he's not tormenting you. He'll be your husband, and he'll provide a good life for you, Wendy. You need this."

My hand hurts even more at the nonchalant way she dismisses my pain. "You're telling me to let him hurt me?"

She shakes her head. "Of course not! It's not like that at all, and you know it. Dreams and made-up stories, they don't have a place when you're an adult. You have to stop telling yourself these fairy tales."

I move to the stairs, just wanting to escape into my room and digest the words she's throwing my way. "So, you knew?"

Mother won't meet my gaze, and instead looks toward the floor, wringing her hands together. "I know Mrs. Davenport has always been fond of you. She'll help take great care of you."

And finally, she meets my eyes. They're full of a strange conflict, and it just makes me angrier.

"So, remembering the 'stories' I made up as a child when we played together, you thought it a good idea to promise me to him?"

She cringes, and I have my answer. When she opens her mouth to speak I hold up a hand.

"Don't even try." The tears I fought so hard against run down my face, dripping onto my dress. "And don't ever think I'll give into this. As long as I can, I will find a way to fight this."

And I take the steps two at a time, the sixth step be damned. I want out of this dress, out of this house and away from this family. After what seems like so many tears, and so much time, I feel this tiny hand tugging at my elbow.

"Wendy?"

I ignore him. Little brothers and their inopportune moments.

"Pweas Wendy? Don't cwy," Michael says and my heart melts.

Without looking I tug him to me and pull him into my lap as I sit up. After a ferocious hug, I pull away, aware my face is probably a red-eyed mess and look at him. Tears stream down his pudgy cheeks, and I suddenly feel horrible for making him worry.

"It's all right, little one," I say and stroke his hair to try and soothe him. "I just hurt myself a little."

His large eyes regard me somberly and he glances at the hand I hold to my chest. "Does it hurt bad?"

I nod, and this time he moves enough to wrap his short arms around my neck. I wish I could explain to him that the physical hurt wasn't really the bad part. It's the hollow space inside now, where I thought I knew the reasons, where I thought I knew how to get out of it and what I wanted to do with my life at least for now.

But as he pats my hair and whispers, "Ever'ting will be a'right, Wendy," while clutching both myself and his teddy bear, all I want to do is break down and never pick up the pieces again.

~

I'm not sure what time it is when I wake, for Michael is still curled in my arms, gently sucking his thumb, and someone draped a blanket around us. It might have been Mother but was more than likely John. I listen to the house around us and blink up at the ceiling, as the total silence around me intensifies in that way it does when you concentrate on it. My parents have probably been in bed for a long time by now.

And I'd been so set on scouting out watch routines after they went to bed. But at this hour, it'll be a waste of time.

I push myself up gently so as not to disturb Michael and sit watching him for a few moments. He's not grown up with as much of Mother's attention as I, or even John did. She's busier now, working on Father's career, because a successful man has a good wife—or something like that.

Michael needs to go back in the nursery, so I stand up, forgetting my right hand for a moment so much that I stifle a scream of pain when I put weight on it hand to push myself up. Tiny black spots dance in from of my eyes for a moment, and I scowl back the outburst. Putting up with that sort of behavior shouldn't be the normal thing to do. It isn't normal at all!

After a few moments the pain recedes and I glance down at it. Strange. In this light it doesn't seem bruised at all. I realize I'm still in my day dress. Suppressing a groan at the thought I unlace the dress and get into one of my nightgowns. It's enough time for my hand to recover a bit too.

I steel myself against bending down and lifting Michael up to carry him back to his room. The pain is manageable if I use my left hand to bear most of the weight. Or it is at first.

By the time I get Michael to the nursery and into his bed, I'm short of breath from pain. I curl up with him, like we used to before I had to move. There's rustling across the way in John's bed and a moment later he stands at the foot of Michael's.

"Were you warm enough?" he asks, his big eyes serious as he squints at me. No matter what, he always forgets to pop his glasses on if he wakes in the middle of the night.

"I knew that was you." Color rises in John's cheeks, and he smiles. "We were perfectly warm, thank you."

And I mean it.

These boys are my treasures. They're my best friends and the ideal I hold up to compare all of the orphanage boys to. But at the same time I now find myself wanting to protect my brothers, to give them the best thing possible, and I'm starting to wonder if bringing them back from Neverland was the best thing to do.

He sits on the edge of Michael's bed and frowns. "Can I...can I curl up too?"

There's a tone to his voice, a worried one, and I know that when he's ready, he'll tell me what's on his mind.

"Of course," I smile at him and pat the pillow next to us. By all appearances, I won't be allowed to keep them close to me for much longer, unless I can find some way to change it for all of us.

TYBALT

It takes three days before I see a definite pattern in the watch's patrols. My mother keeps a stern eye on me, and I think she thinks it's my fault Albert hasn't called on me yet. With any luck my so called "outspoken" behavior might have chased him off. But I don't think Mrs. Davenport is going to give up so easily.

I'm so tired when I finally get back to Stepney that it's difficult to keep my eyes open while preparing the loaves for the boys. I want to share Neverland with them again, but my need for sleep keeps trying to trick my eyelids into closing.

"Wendy?" Mrs. Johnson's voice is so close, I jump. She hesitates a moment as I look at her. "Sorry, dear. Didn't mean to startle ya. Thought you looked tired."

Even as the thoughts run through my head, I calm down. At least now I'm a bit more awake.

"Haven't been sleeping well." I say, trying to apologize without actually saying the words.

She smiles at me and goes about doing what she was. For a while I just watch and wonder how it might have been for her if she'd visited with Peter and the boys.

Neverland still brings me such solace. Carefree with an edge of danger, but no worry about ever growing up. Every time I think of it, an ache forms in my chest. About how I miss the ease of flying, the reality of magic, and the boys that looked up to me so. Perhaps that's why I like the orphanage so much. They are the lost boys of this world, and they need me just like the others did.

And so, as soon as I sit down, and they gather around me, eyes bright with interest. Yearning for the tales, this sense of youth and happiness, washes over me. I smile and receive a dozen smiles in return. It's all I can do though, as I glance around and notice Henry isn't among them, to control that smile and not scowl. I glance at where Thomas stands in the back left corner, pushed in where the shadows almost conceal him. What is it with boys and their shadows? He nods, barely perceptibly and I suddenly feel cold. Poor Henry. I'm taking too long to get them away.

But I switch the smile brighter and lean forward. "Today we'll hear a different tale, one of the Lost Boys and how they came to be."

Silence greets those words, but it's the good kind, and I venture forth, not completely certain that it's true, but for now it'll help me let them understand that they're not alone in this.

"The boys lived in worlds and countries not unlike here in London. You see, they'd lost their parents in accidents, some in sickness." A collective sad sigh. Some of these boys know this story too well. "But instead of a home, they ran away to places like Kensington Gardens, where they met Peter Pan."

The gasp that ripples through the room is delightful. And I continue, weaving the story, with them as the characters. I think some of them realize this as secretive winks are exchanged between one another.

"He asked Tinkerbell to gift them with pixie dust, so that they might fly to Neverland where they'd never grow old, and never grow up. So they flew and made a camp, and had food fights every day without someone yelling at them."

"Did they miss their families?" Joshua pipes up, his meek little voice awash with the tears he refuses to shed.

"Some." I say, nodding gravely. "But now they had a new family, of boys who understood them, of boys just like them. The family of the lost boys."

"I want to be a lost boy!" someone cries, and I smile as I try to pick them out. But soon the whole room is calling it out and laughing and tackling each other.

Thomas claps his hands in three loud bursts, and the noise subsides. "That's all very well, but none of those lost boys will get the food Mrs. Johnson's just put on the dinner table for ya." He winks at them and smiles as they dash to the dining room in a trail of "thank you, Wendy!"

It only takes a few strides for Thomas to be by my side as the boys dash to feed.

"You look so tired." The concern in his voice and the scrunch to his brows makes me feel bad. He worried about me, for me, and all I want to do is tell him everything, but I can't.

Thomas stands there, patiently waiting until I feel I can speak. It's all I can do not to blurt out my whole life's current situation, but I don't, because I'm supposed to be the strong one, the girl with solutions.

"Mother has been keeping me busy at home." It's not a lie, and I don't want it to be. I don't think boys truly care about marriage, outside of that they'll get married.

He raises an eyebrow as if he knows I'm hiding something else, but after a few moments he waves a hand in dismissal and grins at me again. He moves a tad closer and places a hand on my shoulder, looking at me. Too close to me, yet I don't move away.

"I've been taking note of when the watches change and when the patrols are increased, as well as the lamplighter schedules along Commercial Lane."

His breath washes over me, faintly mint like in odor, it ruffles my hair like a gentle breeze I want to lean into. I fear I sound a little breathless when I answer.

"That's excellent. I've got White Horse covered, and I'll make sure the way-house stays empty for a while." I'm quite certain I could find a way to trap some rats or something, if I can figure out how to. Where there's one, there's probably a lot of them. Smell always chases people away. Poor rats.

"Can you stay a while?" Thomas's question takes me by surprise and I blink at him.

"Where?" Does he mean the way-house? Neverland?

He nods, and I notice his hand is still on my shoulder, the warmth welcome and calming. "Just for a little while. Talk to me? Spend some time with me."

It's an offer I want to scream yes to, but what if Mother saw? Will she never allow me to return then? I hesitate and I think he takes it the wrong way, because he removes his hand and cold air gets sucked into the place it occupied, chilling me briefly to the bone.

"Maybe on days Mother isn't here." Thomas shrugs, and for a moment I realize I've injured him. I try to explain. "It's not that I'm ashamed of our friendship, I'm afraid that she'll forbid me from coming back if she sees it."

He smiles, though for an instant a dark cloud settled in his eyes, but it's gone as he squeezes my left hand. "It's all right, Wendy. We're from very different worlds. But I need for you to talk to Tybalt."

I must look confused, because I've definitely talked to Tybalt before. Everyone has. He's rarely quiet.

But Thomas shakes his head. "I want you to talk to him as the person who's going to help free him from his predicament and give him an escape."

"Of course," I say, realizing he wants an answer from me. As I say the words I notice how much I mean it. They fill me with a purpose right down to the unease in my stomach.

So I wait while he fetches Tybalt. He's so full of life with his smart-aleck comments and questions he knows he shouldn't be asking. His opinions are always out there and boisterous. It's such a pity no one has adopted him. He walks up to me with Thomas and grins.

"Tell me a story, Wendy?" he says, and there's this hitch to his voice that almost breaks me down then and there. I refrain and ruffle his hair instead, gripping myself to have the talk.

"I have plenty of stories for you, Ty, you know that." I reach down and give him a hug, unsure as to why my heart appears to be aching, why I feel this strange sense of foreboding running through me at the prospect of sending Tybalt to Neverland. I hate goodbyes, and this will mean never seeing him again.

He looks up at me, suddenly all his youth painfully obvious. Tears line his eyes, and I can see the fight inside him as he tries valiantly to keep them at bay.

"It's alright, Ty." I stroke his hair this time and attempt to make my voice soothing. I can solve his problems, this complete lack of ever having experienced love or family. "How about I take you to a friend of mine? Where you'll never have to steal or be punished again. Where you'll never have to grow up, where you'll never be alone. Where you can remain just as you are now?"

The smile that spreads from ear to ear is my answer, and everything clicks into place.

~

There's a small park near the Stepney that Thomas will help Tybalt hide in until I can get him, later this evening. It's difficult to remain calm while we have dinner, but I do my best to be demure Wendy. Can't have a reason for Mother to keep a closer eye on me.

"Wendy! Tuck us in?" Micahel asks, echoed by John.

"Please, tell us a story?"

I force the smile onto my face, but really it could be in my best interests. "Of course, Mother, may we be excused?"

"Yes, dear," she says a little distractedly.

"I'll pop straight to bed myself. I've had such a busy day." I try to make sure she knows I'll be asleep, but my plan almost backfires.

Mother looks up and frowns this time. "You are looking a little worn out, Wendy. Perhaps you should take a break from the orphanage. Can't have you running yourself down in such an important time as this."

Again with the forced smile, I simply shake my head. "I just need a good night's sleep."

She nods and waves me away. "Then shoo, and make sure you get one."

I tuck both boys in, and settle down to read them a quick story. Even as I speak, I notice how my brothers are clean of smudges and markings, how their fair skin and sparkling hair only makes the bruises I've seen on Tybalt and the others burn deeper in my mind.

As I finish the tick-tock croc and watch their sleepy eyes battling to stay awake, I lean over to hug each of them. Their night clothes are fresh and smell faintly of powder. Nanna is curled up under their window, as if warding off any more night visits from Peter or others like him. My brothers are safe. My brothers are loved. And my brothers will never want for anything.

The chill that runs up my spine as I close their door makes me shudder, and I carefully make my way down the hall. My parents won't be up too much longer, and I do have things to prepare. As soon as I'm in my room I start pulling out one of the smocks that I hid and find some slip-on shoes that are more comfortable. I light a small candle just outside my window, our telltale sign that I need Peter, Tinkerbell, or one of them to come tonight. After I've padded my bed with a few spare pillows I took from the nursery and settled one of my dolls as the head with hair very similar to mine, I hear my parent's walking through the foyer. I can only hope this will fool them if they check on me.

I sneak downstairs, avoiding the pesky step and out of the kitchen entrance. Hurrying up the road, I hear the local church clock striking nine o'clock and Big Ben echoing in the distance, and I know I'll be cutting it close.

Eying the bushes as I walk past the park we agreed on, I spot Tybalt nestled in them at the edge of the path. He reaches out for and grabs my hand as I come past, and I pull him with me, this nervous twinge wringing my gut as we make our way toward the way-house.

His hand is cool, and I feel guilty for making him wait so long, but there's no other option unless I take him there beforehand, and today there wasn't time.

Navigating in the late twilight is just as bad as pitch dark. Taking the route around the back of the church means we might risk running into more parishioners. I should have dressed as an adult, and given them less reason to question me. Not many people down this end of our lane will know my parents, but some might.

It's difficult not to jump at every shadow. I squeeze poor Tybalt's hand a few times, probably a little too hard.

"Is it very far, Wendy?" he asks, and I can hear the way he tries to keep his own misgivings at bay.

I grin down at him. "Not too much farther."

But I barely bite back a shriek in time as something drops in front of us, sending shadows skittering everywhere. Tybalt has no such compunctions and screeches, ducking behind me to hide.

"Mrrrrooowww."

Silly cat.

"It's a cat," I say, and start to laugh softly.

Tybalt creeps out from behind me and stares as the animal saunters away.

"I knew that," he murmurs and starts chuckling too.

The rest of the way passes luckily without incident and I pull him close as we enter the way-house's path.

"Stay close to me," I whisper as the door opens easily, and he clutches his hands in my skirts, suddenly much younger than he's ever seemed. We walk to the top of the cellar stairs and though it's so dark, faint moonlight escapes into us through the window. For the first time since beginning this, I hesitate.

"Are you sure you want to do this?"

Tybalt nods, and suddenly a bit of panic rises in my stomach and I kneel in front of him, hands clenching his upper arms and bringing him eye to eye with me.

"Once we start this, they won't let you back. You'll never come back. Do you understand?"

He nods, and in the dim light I can see a flash of fear through his expression, but he gathers courage I wish I could borrow and nods yet again. "To Neverland, right?"

"To Neverland." I repeat, hug him tight and lead him down the stairs.

Tybalt drinks the tea dutifully, like the others did too.

"That's really sweet," he says, crinkling up his nose. "Better than bitter, though."

He grins and I tousle his hair as he lets himself fall back into the cushions, arms splayed to the side.

I'm tempted to drink some of the tea myself, but I don't need to. Now we wait. I lean back against the wall, watching him squirm a little on the pillows. Slowly but surely, he just curls up and lies contently amidst all of them. I'm so glad it's comfortable. If I let myself lie down though, I'll never stand back up in time.

I'm not sure how much time passes while I watch him, waiting for them to arrive, but I think I almost fall asleep.

Peter's hand on my shoulder, gently shaking me, brings me back to the room. I blink in the dim light to see the candles have melted quite a bit. They're late. I'll have to wake Tybalt up before we go. He looks so peaceful I wish I didn't have to.

As I shake him, I realize he's still cool, like he was outside. Silly me, I should have covered him with a blanket. But his huge eyes look up at me, a strange quiet desperation in them, like this is his only option. I hug him and motion Peter over.

"This is Tybalt. He's a lot like John, except he talks more."

Except he's here, in need of saving, but I don't add that part.

Peter smiles and jumps into the air, flexing his lack of arm muscles and grinning from ear to ear. I roll my eyes and think that Thomas would never do something silly like that. And then I'm left to wonder why I'm thinking of Thomas at all right here and now.

The jingling of Tinkerbell's laugh reaches my ears, and I see her up high near the slit of the window they'll have to squeeze through. She's waiting, and Peter beckons to her. With a lot of ringing in my ears and a horrible scowl-like pout on her adorable little face, she lets him shake her just a bit over Tybalt.

Tink always makes me feel so inferior. Her pint-sized perfection, that beautiful glow surrounding her, and the bit of faerie chatter only Peter ever seems to be able to understand. I'm still not sure why she showed me that tea, but our relationship is, at best, strained. I think I'll always keep my distance.

Peter is standing directly over me.

"What?" I'm proud not to stammer as I speak to him.

He grins, that little upturned pug nose scrunching up as he laughs outright. "I was asking you if you have the energy for a visit, Wendy Darling!"

I blink at him, and the smile I'm quite sure encompasses most of my face slowly makes my jaw ache with the effort. "Yes!"

I didn't think they'd ever take me back. Maybe if they take me once, they'll take me again.

The golden dust falls around my head and onto my shoulders, enveloping me softly in a way I'd forgotten in all but my dreams. I take Tybalt's hand and squeeze it gently.

"It's all right," I say to him. "Everything is going to be all right."

Several moments pass as I look him in the eyes, until I'm certain that lost look is gone. He'll be fine. They all will. I just know it.

The window is all but too small, and I'm quite certain I hear my skirts rip, but am beyond caring. There's this small voice in the back of my head telling me to run, to fly and never come back. To let this Albert mess and my father sort themselves out. But that horribly logical part of myself is too responsible. Dislike my situation though I might, I can't leave my brothers to fend for themselves. I can't leave my mother and father thinking their daughter has disappeared. Besides, there are other boys needing my help.

Then there's Thomas. I didn't realize how much I'd miss him.

~

The wind is chill and I'm glad I wore my shawl again. Up high like we are, there's always more bite. It doesn't take long to transition, and it's expected this time, anticipated even. I've been here before, done it all. The islands below us are magnificently familiar, ships in the water, coves with hidden treasures. How I can't wait to see the lost boys again.

This skycap is so open and distant, free from parental intervention, free to be who we are and what we want to be, with that added bonus of eternal childhood. It's airy and spacious, never-ending horizons that give limitless possibilities I'll never have the chance to grasp for myself. All I can do is send the boys here, to live with the other lost boys, where they never have to think about growing old or having adults hurt them and tear their dreams apart.

Little has changed in the cove when we get there. Though the trees are bigger, with more leaves for coverage. The boys are all the same. Boisterous and laughing, eating and drinking. It's what they do, because they never have to worry about someone telling them not to.

Tybalt takes it all in, a smile slowly spreading on his face as he barely glances back at me before diving into the fray of likeminded boys. A pain sits in the center of my chest, like someone kicked me. It hurts to watch him leave, to know I won't see him again.

For a little while, I just want to watch them all—all of these lost boys enjoying the lives they couldn't have had without Neverland. Enjoying this time over and over, forever and always, because growing up is overrated. Growing up is something you have to do on the mainland. I see David and James a little to the rear, their eyes reflecting the dancing flames.

Sitting in the shadow of the great tree, a tear snakes down my cheek before I realize quite how upset I am. I keep my eyes on Tybalt and Peter and I can see their hair sway gently in the breeze as it rolls in off the water, and yet it fails to brush my face. Bitterness taints the back of my throat as I force myself to swallow. This isn't my home, and as much as I have fond memories, as much as I wish it could be, it never will be.

I content myself to watch for what will be the last time—I can feel it in my bones. The smiles on their faces light up the hollow as they all dance to silly ditties and play fight amongst themselves. Tybalt fits right in. Sometimes, as I blink, in a trick of the campfire for just a moment, his laughter seems like a grimace and the color leaks out of the visage before me leaving the cheerful scene grey and desolate, cold and unforgiving as the light refracts strangely.

Am I really giving the boys a better possible future? Is this grey alternative a glimpse of what truly awaits them? Have I misunderstood what Neverland is?

But in the next blink it's gone, and the campfire cackles merrily, mocking my strange interruption of the happiness, dancing, and food. This is where I turn to, and if there's no other recourse, this is where I'll run to.

TRUTHS

The room is dim when I wake, and it takes a couple of moments for me to orientate myself. A dank stench briefly fills my nostrils, causing me to gag for a moment. As I roll over trying to fight the retching my twisting stomach demands, I realize I'm on a pile of cushions, and the floor underneath my face is dirt and stone.

Suddenly the smell vanishes. The only illumination comes from what I assume are early dawn rays coming through the one tiny window in this cellar. Please just be the dawn. Mother is going to kill me. I scramble up, rethinking the wisdom of this cushion bed. They don't seem like the best idea anymore, now that they're hindering my every move. Eventually I make it, smooth down my hair with a tiny bit of water left in the urn, and try to shake out my dress as I take the steps back up to the house two at a time.

Not until I make it outside do I dare to look toward the horizon. Relief floods through me as I realize they truly are the first rays of morning. I've not missed the day.

Yet.

As fast as I can without looking suspicious, I walk home, hoping my dress doesn't look like I slept on a pile of cushions in a cellar. Mother won't approve of this dress. It's plain cotton, and dark, and probably the roughest material I own. There's barely any shape to it, much like the smocks I used to wear not too long ago.

Our house is still mostly in shadow when I tiptoe in the back entrance, thankfully avoiding Joan, even though I'm quite certain I hear her rummaging around in the pantry. With speed born of practice I fly up the stairs, skillfully avoiding that pesky sixth one. Better not push my luck by making the stairs creak louder than a cannon.

Almost to my room, I heave a sigh of relief as I place my hand on the doorknob.

"Wendy!"

Oh. No. I fight back the heat I feel behind my eyelids and try to stop my shoulders from shaking before I turn to face Mother.

She's not as close as I thought she was, and I bite down a sigh of relief. "Yes, Mother?"

"You're not going to wear that today, are you?"

Biting back the laughter threatening to bubble out of my throat, I shrug and try my best to feign innocence. "This? What's wrong with this? I thought you like me in blue."

"What am I going to do with you," she mutters the not-question under her breath, ushering me back into my room. "Sit down. I'll go over dress etiquette again."

As I sit and watch her rifle through my dresses, I attempt to swallow the huge yawn I feel coming on, and fail abysmally.

"Wendy, that's not ladylike at all. Did you get no sleep?" She leans closer and frowns as she scrunches her nose. Gripping a tiny bit of my skirt, she brings it up to her face and scowls. "What's that smell? This smells horrendous. Can't you tell? Are you ill?"

I shake my head. "No. No. Just a little tired."

"Tired and apparently bereft of a sense of smell. Get that off. We'll burn it. I don't think anything is going to get that smell out." She waits, right there, while I strip down to my slip and tosses the dress through the door out into the hallway. "Really, we try to give you everything, and you insist on wearing clothing that smells like a dark, rotting, vegetable patch."

The cellar. I could punch myself if she wouldn't notice the action.

Sleeping in those cushions probably made the dress reek. I just knew there were rats down there, and I'll have to do something about the musty smell.

"Sorry, Mother." The apology is instinctual, borne in me since I can remember. Always make sure you say sorry to Mother, especially when you're unsure why. Father taught me that, even if he didn't mean to.

But she's not paying attention to me anymore as she looks through and dismisses almost everything in my closet. I still don't understand why she bought me so many dresses. They cost a fortune, and I don't understand this overwhelming importance she places on appearance.

"Ah," she says with this strange hitch of reverence in her voice. "I like this one."

She turns around to me, dress in hand.

About to object, just because I usually object to the outfits Mother picks out for me, I stop in my tracks, unable to actually formulate what I was going to say. Mainly because I think I like the one she has draped over her arm for once. Standing up, I tentatively run a finger over it. It's this sheer navy blue over a pale pink undercoat. There's no corset in this—it's the newer, more daring fashion. It'll sit just under my bust line, gathered with a little velvet bow and roses, and the skirts will fall down to swish against my feet. The sleeves are short and only cover the upper part of my arms, while the neckline will run easily from shoulder to shoulder.

"Do you like it?" Mother whispers to me, reminding me fleetingly of how Thomas speaks to me when he doesn't want anyone to hear. I wonder if Thomas will like this dress.

"Isn't it too nice to wear out today?" I ask hesitantly. I want to wear it.

She shrugs at me and smiles. "I think you're old enough to be careful while you wear it. I'm sure it'll still be fine for company this afternoon. And besides, you really look like you could do with a day of feeling pretty." Mother leans forward and takes my shoulders in her hands, looking me in the eye, before cupping my face and kissing me on the cheeks.

"I know sometimes it may not seem like it, but I do really try to make things work for you. Always. I will always try to give you the best." She gives me a fierce hug, one that brings the distant memories from when I was so tiny crashing back. Her arms have this quality, this safe haven sensation that nothing on this earth will ever equal, yet again, the very last thing I want to do is grow up. She pulls away, and I think I see a tear in her eye before she hurriedly rubs it away. "Now indulge me and get dressed so I can see just how perfect this is on you."

I watch as she leaves the room. It's strange for her to leave me to get dressed once she's chosen an outfit. Signs of growing up, or else she's just preoccupied. Last night was so bittersweet, so full of memories and jealousy I feel about never being able to go there again. Though Neverland trumps everything, sometimes being here isn't so bad.

I'm so tired I can barely stand up, and slipping into this dress is more difficult than I thought it'd be. Sleeping on a bed of haphazardly arranged cushions isn't good for me. My back hurts a little, like I've dragged something heavy a great distance. Cushions do not a bed make.

Finally, I think I've wrangled myself into the gown. Gown because I don't feel like dress is the correct term, and now I'm worried about dirtying it before this evening. This evening. Oh no. The dress was a distraction from the fact that they'll be coming. I know it's them; why else would we have guests? I so hope he's found something else to catch his attention.

I'm sure Mother is outside the door, and my hands just won't work with their half-numb fingers as I try to draw the ribbons on the back closed.

"Mother." I say it softly, not entirely sure I want her to come in. Once she does the back up, I'm sealed inside this dress. This dress, I actually like. What is happening to me?

She pushes the door open, and another tear snakes down her cheek, but this time she doesn't try to wipe it away. Is she that happy I like the dress? Maybe I've been too hard on her. It's not Mother's fault

I like to think for myself. Or perhaps it is, since she raised me to think I could. I'm proud of myself and the things I want to accomplish, even if no one but the boys will ever know about them.

"You look beautiful, Wendy. Make sure to wear an apron today, and don't dally after you read to the boys. When you get home, we'll help you put your hair up." She smiles and hugs me again.

This much attention is a bit overwhelming. I'm unused to all of these hugs and smiles, this laughter and nicer side of my mother. She hasn't been this way since I was tiny, and suddenly I feel truly guilty.

"I do love you, Mother," I blurt out before I've had a chance to think the words through.

Her eyes open a little wider and the smile that spreads across her face warms my heart. "I know, but thank you for saying so. Sometimes it's nice to hear."

She pets my now yellow-mottled hand, apparently oblivious to the bruising, and I grimace slightly.

Maybe she'll be willing to listen. On impulse I reach out and catch her hand, squeezing it in my own. "Is it set, Mother? This thing—is there no way you'll consider allowing me to wait for someone else?"

She looks at me, and for a few moments all the warmth drains from her face, and the wrinkles and crow's feet around her eyes make their weary appearance. I drop her hand and take a step back, wishing I could retract the words too, wishing I hadn't shown my vulnerability, or broken this rare moment of trust between us.

"Wendy Darling. Who would you meet?" Her tone is soft, and sad, and very, very tired. "Where would you meet them if not through us? Life isn't just helping out at the orphanage. Life isn't a faerie tale."

She hits so close to home with the last phrase. How does she know me so well when everything I've done has been to hide it from her? To hide it from everyone?

"No." I don't know what to say, because there is no answer. Peter has never been a true possibility, as much as I'd like to think so. But Thomas? He's equally as out of reach, when class distinction means so much.

She sits down on my bed and pats at her hair. "As much as you might think so, love, we aren't doing this to harm you. I'm doing this to make sure you're taken care of. Albert's family is rich and can open so many doors for you."

I've never heard Mother plead with me before, like she's willing me to understand and forgive their motivations. For a moment I almost want to. She's good. "He's not worth any of it. I'd prefer to live in the gutter than end up with someone like him."

"Is he really so bad?" she asks, this strange half-smirk to her face.

I blink at her and hold out my right hand with its faintly mottled yellow bruising still visible. "Yes. He's really so bad, and I'm sure he'll do worse things."

Mother stands up and walks to me, her lips downturned now and real sadness reflected in her eyes. "I wish you'd stop that, Wendy. Stop insisting these wrongs you fabricate are real."

"Do I have to marry?" I ask and really have to stop speaking before I think.

She laughs for a moment. "You don't understand, Wendy. Your father and I could barely afford children. We have worked very hard to give you all good lives, but there comes a point, like it did for us, when you need to grow up and leave the nest. In your case, you'll be someone else's care, in the boys, it'll be up to them to support them-selves and their wives. You understand, yes?"

But I don't, even though I nod the opposite. "But can't I," I choke out, and my mother holds up her hand to stall me.

"We love you, Wendy." She leans forward and gives me a small kiss on my head before heading to the door and looking back. "Just give Albert another chance, please. He might be working the last of his juvenile inclinations out." She pauses, frowning. "Put on some of that rose water before you come down. That horrible smell is lingering a little. It's going to be a great day, sweetheart."

The door closes behind her, and I count to ten, hoping she doesn't come back through the door. When I hit eleven, my body is still shak-ing. It takes a few seconds for me to calm down but when I do, the answer is clear in my mind. All I have to do now is work out the details of my plan.

BREAKDOWN

Only the sound of the horses clopping down the street and the strange puttering whirr of those newfangled vehicles accompanies us as we walk to Stepney this morning. And I let my mind wander to those carriage contraptions. They mention horse power in conjunction with them. I wonder if it's truly the ghosts of past horses pulling them, or if they mean something else.

Mother stops abruptly, just before our turn. "Go ahead. Tell Mrs. Johnson that I have preparations to make for tonight and expect you home in a timely manner." She stands, poised, waiting for my answer.

I nod. The glum feeling sinks to the bottom of my stomach, letting queasiness abound, and I say, "Yes, Mother," because I think she expects something verbal.

It's not until the words are out that she looks satisfied and turns back toward our house.

For a few minutes I wonder if she'll notice if I run. She'd never find me in Neverland. Wouldn't even know where to start looking. But who would Michael and John turn to? Mother and Father no longer have time for that, and Joan has far too many responsibilities. Maybe Nanna would hear them, but the dear old girl is getting older. One day she won't be around anymore at all.

The sun beats down on me in my blue finery, yet unease makes my stomach churn. Everything is spiraling out of control.

At least I can still help the boys. I can teach them and tell them stories. Maybe even of last night, if I can gather those thoughts properly. First things though. I clutch the basket of bread tightly and turn down the path. Even in this bright morning, the buildings tower over me, their shadows extending to steal away the sunlight and leave me in their desolate wake. I've never had to take such a huge breath to walk up that entrance, but I manage it. Especially since I know the boys are waiting—not only for their bread, but for their story, that one glimpse of hope.

Mrs. Johnson greets me at the door and happily relieves me of the basket. "I was wondering when you'd get here. A little later than usual this morning, miss."

Her friendly chatter does little to assuage my bleak mood. All I can muster is a half smile in response to her banter.

She frowns, and after putting the bread basket somewhere safe, dusts her hands off and gently tugs my shoulder around until I face her. "Here, Miss Wendy. Are you feeling all right?"

For the few moments it takes my brain to process the words, I stare at her and the lines around her eyes, eyes that twinkle regardless of how difficult her path has been. Suddenly I want to shake her and ask her why she won't believe the boys, why she won't take time to hear their plight. Though maybe she too has her own Albert. I purse my lips and resist the urge to hug her, to throw my arms around this woman who technically has so much less than I do and just cry.

Instead, I draw myself up, take a deep breath and smile as best I can. "I'm fine, really. Just didn't get enough sleep."

"Ah," Mrs. Johnson says, and it's obvious from the raised eyebrow that she doesn't believe a word I just said. "No sleep'll do that to ya. Just you mind, miss, we need you here. The boys love you. We'd 'ate to see you get sick."

This time my smile is real and the renewed warmth banishes the chill. "Thank you, Mrs. Johnson." I truly hope she can see how much I mean it, because her little pep talk is exactly what I needed to hear right now.

The rest of the morning passes quickly, and I realize I've forgotten to give the lady my mother's message. I pull her to one side.

"Sorry to bother you, Mrs. Johnson. But Mother wanted me to tell you to make sure I don't head home too late, since she has preparations for tonight to take care of." I think I got some of the message garbled, but overall, I'm sure the gist of it was there.

There's this brief flash of something through Mrs. Johnson's eyes, but it's gone just as quick. I think it might have been pity, and I'm not sure how I feel about that.

"It's all right, pet," she says and pats my hand gently. "We'll make sure you get home on time."

She takes me by the shoulders and steers me toward the door. "Now you go do what you really came to do. Give me that apron, and go tell the boys one of your stories. One that'll 'ave them all laughing for the rest of the day and make them feel like there's a bit of 'ope left in the world, eh?"

She's gone before I can reply. I square my shoulders, lift my chin, and walk into the room.

～

The boys are the boys; only Tybalt and Henry are missing. And while Tybalt's absence is obvious to me, I don't think it fazes anyone else, not yet. I have to steal a moment for myself to quash the anger rising in the back of my throat. That it's commonplace not to notice as soon as a boy goes missing just makes me want to kick things. But at least for me Tybalt's smiling face and flushed cheeks are sorely absent in what now seems like a very dull and grey room.

Telling them stories about last night, about the night Tybalt left them all behind, feels callous and cruel. It makes me so sad I have to fight back the burn behind my eyes and ignore it lest I cry hot tears. So I just tell them my tale again. How Peter found our nursery, and how my brothers and I came to visit Neverland. How Tinkerbell never really liked me, or any of us, jealous as she was of Peter's friendship, and how we indeed came to meet the lost boys who were all lost in so many different ways.

I didn't mean for the story to be so sobering, and though none of them cry, it's a very somber bunch that heads off to lunch. As I watch them file out to eat, I don't even realize Thomas is next to me until he brushes his fingers along my elbow.

Startled, I jump and when I see it's him, it's all I can do not to break down and cry. I'm stronger than this. It's just the fatigue of barely sleeping the last few nights.

"Wendy? What's wrong? Did something go wrong last night?"

I shake my head and raise an eyebrow. "Not last night. You'd have heard, silly. My life...it's just not really my own right now."

I don't know why I'm telling Thomas of all people, but I can't keep things bottled up inside like this.

"Mother and Father have chosen a husband for me."

"What?" Thomas's eyes open big as saucers, and his jaw slacks a bit, leaving his mouth gaping open.

"They've chosen someone I've known most of my life to be my husband. For me to spend the rest of my life with. He's rich. They say that's a good thing for me. I'll have a great life." I sit on my chair, but can't stay still, so I stand. Then I pace because I feel like my body is on fire.

"So you know him? Isn't that good then?" Thomas's tone catches me off guard. It's like he's trying to reason with me and maybe with himself.

"No." I shake my head, because I don't want to hear the lecture from him, definitely not from him. "No, it's not. It's terrible, because I know what he's like. I know the side he never showed the adults."

A shudder wracks my frame and I wrap my arms around my chest in a type of hug. Maybe I can ward things out that way.

"What side?"

"It's cruel and it's mean, and he knows how to manipulate everyone. I'm trying to come up with a way out, but proving to my mother that he's horrible hasn't worked. She said things are just that way." I sit, this time needing to catch my breath. I can't believe how worked up I'm getting. This can all be dealt with later, I have far too much to do right now.

"Wendy." There's pity in his voice, in his eyes, in the way he tries to whisper my name to calm me down. I don't want pity, from anyone. Not my mother. Not Mrs. Johnson. And definitely not Thomas.

"It's fine," I say and bat at his hands as he bends down in front of me. "I will be all right. Sorry. I shouldn't have mentioned anything."

"Don't be silly," he says and wipes a tear from my cheek that I didn't even realize I'd shed.

For that tiny moment, I lean into the warmth of his calloused hands. Honest hands. Hands that help and don't hurt. Hands that don't make me sick when they touch my skin.

I look up at him as he pulls me to stand with him, my hands against his chest, and I wonder his expression is so soft, the faint smile tugging at his lips.

"I'm not being silly." I mutter feebly.

"Yes, you are. Why do you think I wouldn't want to listen to you? You spend hours reading these kids an escape, and lately you've spent ages trying to provide them with one. Why ever would I not listen?" His green eyes have dropped down a shade, to this warm and gentle green. While I've always known Thomas was a bit different than the other boys here, I never really had proof.

My chest feels like a sack of stone has lifted, and suddenly I'm so tired. Not only is the lack of sleep while in Neverland the night before catching up to me, but the sheer relief of telling someone what I'm going through is overwhelming. I sink down into the old, worn chair and rest my head against the back. Thomas takes a few steps and stands beside me.

"Can you tell me things a little clearer maybe?" He speaks softly, probably so his voice doesn't carry and get him called into the dining area because I know if he's not careful, he's going to miss his lunch.

But I want to talk to him, want to tell him everything that's on my mind, even the trivial things. "My father's boss has a son, a little older than myself. I've known him since we were children, and our parents met for tea frequently. But he's always had this mean streak, beating turtles, kicking puppies—that sort of thing."

"And your mother doesn't believe you?"

For a moment I contemplate just pulling the brave face back over and laughing it off, but instead, I shake my head. "Not like that. She believes these are my stories—"

"Stories?"

"Mother says this is to take care of me, and that they're doing this for my own good. Why can't I look after myself? I'm not weak or slow-witted. I'm strong and determined, clever and resourceful when needed. I don't want to be taken care of."

In the next moment Thomas has enveloped me in a hug. A horrible breach of protocol if my mother were to see it. And as the shock wears off, I realize how much I don't mind it. I've needed this contact, this sense of someone believing in me for so long. I hug him back before I pull away.

Putting myself at arms' length I smile, my genuine smile because he deserves nothing less. "Thank you. I really needed that."

A faint tint of color creeps higher in his cheeks, as if he doesn't believe the audacity he had to do what he just did. And that's probably what he's feeling. "Sorry, you just really look like you needed comfort, and I didn't know what to say."

"It's all right. Really, Thomas. I feel so much calmer now."

"Good!" He rubs his hands together, eyes sparkling again. "So now we have to plan a few things."

"We?" I cross my arms and look him dead in the eye. "And what might we be planning, sir?"

Thomas grins. "Well first up, we have a few more boys we need to ferry over. And after that I believe we have a plan to devise."

"What sort of plan?" I play along even though a part of me is hoping that he means an Albert plan.

"If your parents won't listen to reason, then we need to get you out of there. Since we've become so adept at sneaking boys out of the home, and through to Neverland, we should be able to sneak you away, and have enough time to put good distance between us." His lips curve in a mischievous expression and I can't help but be caught up in his courageous suggestion.

Who says we can't do this? Who says I can't be my own person? They're fighting for the right to vote in the middle of London, really not far away at all. That's who I want to be, if I have to stay here in this world of growing up.

I nod, because I realize I've got carried away with my thoughts while he's waiting for an answer. "Boys to Neverland, and then we examine our options."

Thomas nods, and I think the thought of us running away makes him happy. Maybe the hug meant as much to him as it did to me. I don't think I'm successful in fighting the heat I can feel rising in my cheeks.

"Think on a plan, and we'll go into more detail when I come next time," I say as I begin to gather my things.

"You're going already?" His expression droops so much—I feel bad for having to go.

I nod and gather my book and re-pin my hat. "Mother needs me home tonight. Just let me know which boy is next, and I'll take him in the next few nights."

Thomas nods and reaches out tentatively to pat my arm. "You just be careful. Watch out for yourself, and remember, we'll get you out of this ridiculous situation."

As I pull away the warmth of his hand lingers against my skin, and I'm glad he saw me in this dress first.

"It's a deal," I say as I head out of the room.

So many ideas whirl through my head, but one sticks at the forefront, a thought I can't share with Thomas until I'm completely certain. As much as my gut tells me it's a bad idea, maybe I can find a way to take us both to Neverland.

DINNER

I always lose track of time when talking to Thomas. I do make it back with plenty of time in my own eyes, just not my mother's.

The stern smile on her face barely qualifies as one, and all the enthusiasm I managed to work up back at the orphanage leaks away from me, through the cracks in the wooden floor. She doesn't speak a word until the door closes and she takes the basket out of my hands.

"I thought we understood each other this morning, Wendy." But she doesn't sound angry. There's this overwhelming tone of disappointment in her voice. Anger wouldn't make me feel so guilty.

"We did, Mother. The story went overtime." It's not the excuse she wants, but it's what I have, and she can't really admonish me for doing something worthy with my time when she's the one who insisted I begin volunteering.

"Just pay more attention next time? At least it's not a total disaster. It seems you managed to keep your dress clean. But your hair—" She scowls briefly.

Again with the disappointment. Can't she just be angry and yell? The quiet resignation doesn't suit her. "I know. Joan will be helping me with it, won't she? You said so this morning."

I try to smile softly and push some hopefulness into it, but since I'm not prone to practicing smiles, I have no idea if I've succeeded.

For a moment she forgets to control her features, and her eyebrow shoots up in surprise. "Yes, Joan will be up shortly to help you do your hair. Thank you for coming home early enough."

"Of course. I apologize for not making it earlier." I turn to go up the steps, but she catches my elbow and turns me toward her.

"I'm sorry you got the rough end this morning, Wendy. I had a bad night. Please don't ever think we don't love you. We just do what we have to do, what is needed of us, and what is best for all of us. I know it's difficult to understand at your age, it was for me too." She holds my gaze for a few painstakingly long moments, as if doing so will wash away any memory of her hurtful remarks that morning. Then she bites her lip, and for a moment I think I can see her vulnerability cascading out of it, on show for me to understand. "I should never get angry with you for wanting your own things, but that's just something you'll have to realize is a series of checks and balances. All right?"

She's older than me, but that doesn't mean she wasn't my age once, I guess. All grown up now, with children of her own. Oh, how I don't want to be that. Not that I don't love children, just that I don't want to grow up. A few seconds pass before I find an answer I think she'll accept.

"I know you mean well, but I hope you don't expect me to just accept a fate that's handed to me. You didn't raise me that way."

Her smile disappears and she sighs, and when she speaks there's a hitch to her voice. "No, you're right. I suppose we didn't. Run along and get ready. They'll be here soon."

As I walk up the stairs, I turn around the banister and can still see her standing there, biting her bottom lip as she tries to deal with the conversation we just had. It's the first time in my life I realize that we've had a conversation almost on equal footing, and the fear begins to set, tingling the bottom of my feet and up through my body. Is it too late? Maybe I've already aged too much.

When I reach my room, Michael is sitting on my bed, teddy dangling out of his right hand, its leg trailing far below on the floor.

He's stretched across, one arm theatrically thrown across his eyes, while the other clutches his security toy.

"Michael. What are you doing in my room?" I try to sound stern, and think I almost succeed until I see him grinning from underneath his haphazardly-arranged pose.

He sighs and pushes himself up onto an elbow to look at me, eyes drooping in feigned sadness. This should be good.

"Wendy. You never come and play wif' me anymore." He pouts the words out, if that's possible, with this plaintive tone that manages to seep into the very core of my being.

I laugh, because it's far too cute not to. "Well. You still have John to play with. You remember? Glasses, about yea tall?" I hold out my hand measuring height around my shoulders, and Michael drops his character for a moment. Laughter peals out from between his lips and he rolls on my bed for a moment before reverting back to his previous stance.

"Of course I remember John. Silly," he says, still pulling his facial features back from the smile splitting laugh.

"Then why do you need me to come and play with you?" I ask, gently sitting next to him and pulling him into my lap.

"Because I miss you, Wendy."

Tears well in my eyes, and I don't even sense the burning first. It hits me all at once. I hug my little brother tightly and whisper in his ear. " I miss you too, Michael."

He clings to me, arms flung around my neck, like he'll never let go. "Why did you have to move out? Why can't I come and stay in here wif' you?"

I hug him some more and pry his little fingers from me to settle him more sedately on my lap. "Because I'm growing up."

Even as I speak the words, they sound entirely alien to me, as if there's someone else in my body, admitting something to my little brother that I'm in complete denial about.

"Why do you want to grow up? Remember the fun the lost boys had?" Beseeching eyes nearly rip out my soul.

Of course I remember, but Michael doesn't understand how this world works. I don't even understand it and I'm almost old enough to experience the nasty things.

"I don't want to, Michael, but it's something I have to do. In the end, we all have to grow up."

He wriggles so hard, I almost drop him and stands, hands on his hips, glaring at me. "No, we don't. None of us have to grow up. We could just fly away with Peter, like you've always told us about—we could stay with Peter. Why did you make us come home?"

Without another word, he stomps out of my room, leaving me gaping at his retreating back. Cold forms in the middle of my chest, and I hug myself. I didn't know how strongly they felt; I thought they both wanted the family back. The only thing is, I'm not sure why now that I have the chance to send them back and to go back myself, why I can't bring myself to do so.

The few seconds it takes me to process my little brother's anger and figure out how to tell him why I won't change what we did when I'm not entirely sure why now myself is enough time for Joan to walk up the stairs and make her way to my room. Little boys make no sense, at least my little brothers don't. I'm far better at trying to figure out how the boys at the home will react.

"Miss, your mother says we need to get your hair done." Joan is lovely. Her light brown eyes always highlight the pale blue of her uniform, and the wisps of hair that valiantly try to escape the little white cap she always wears are sort of sweet.

"I know," I say, and seat myself in front of the dresser. Thoughts run rampant in my head while she teases and works on my hair, trying to make it fashionable. It's not something I really care about, so I trust her to know what she's doing.

I have times to sort out in my head, when to get the boys to the way-house, when to notify Peter that I'll have more for him. It's probably better for my state of mind if I don't go with them again. The after effects are bitterness and jealousy. There's something missing when I'm there and missing when I'm here. Either way, I can't seem to win. But what if I could talk to Peter and arrange for Thomas to come too? Wouldn't I have everything then?

By the time Joan's finished, I barely even resemble the me I remember. My hair tumbles in ways I know are only possible because of the pins digging into my head. There's rouge on my cheeks and a pink sheen to my lips. I feel naked even with all these clothes, vulnerable to their gazes and perceptions and beholden to their plots and plans, regardless of the strength I'm trying to muster to fight them.

~

*M*y mother smiles at me as I walk down the stairs, and Father's gasp—even though he quickly hides it—is enough to make my smile genuine.

"You look amazing," he says as he steps forward and takes my hand, squeezing my fingers in the process.

For this moment I can remember the father who tossed me up in the air in a house much smaller than this, who held me as I stumbled through a park nowhere near where we live now.

The father I adored and idolized, who has grown ever more distant since Michael was born. I'm not sure what it is, this whole parental withdrawal thing, but I don't ever want to do it. If I were to grow up and have children, I want them to remember me fondly, love me, and never want to choose to stay somewhere far away from them just because they don't want to go home.

"Are they here yet?" I ask, trying to keep my voice level.

Father shakes his head. "They'll be here shortly. We thought it best to greet them at the door."

I take a shaky breath and swallow, choosing to nod since I can't trust my voice.

But he looks at me with an expression I can't read, like he knows I don't really want to agree yet can't commiserate with me, and he can't help what's happening now that it's been set in motion without severe consequences.

The awkwardness is interrupted by the knock on the door, and the ushering of the Davenport family into the house. I close my eyes briefly to nail down the nausea I feel, the nerves and the fear. When I open them, Albert is striding toward me as my father backs away. But I don't offer my hand, not this time, I simply bow my head slightly in a shallow curtsy and keep an eye on him.

Albert sweeps a majestic bow in front of me, raising an eyebrow as he notices my distinct refusal to offer my hand.

"Delightful to see you again, my lady," he says, with a pompous flair to each syllable and the same hollow and emotionless echo to each word.

At a loss of how to respond, I simply attempt to smile. "Thank you."

I don't want to be rude, but I can't bring myself to return his sentiments in verbal form. Though I can see my mother's frown, it's not as angry as I thought it would be. Instead, I think she's resigned to my rebellion even in this form.

Apparently my words are enough, and Albert falls into step as we all make our way to the dining room. His scent is woody, with a slight hint of sweat. It makes me wonder what he's been up to, who he's been tormenting.

"Do you still volunteer?" he asks after escorting me to a window seat and bringing me a drink of fruit punch.

"Yes," I reply, sipping my drink and wracking my brains for something to say that doesn't involve screaming at him to go away and leave me alone. "I help prepare meals and give the boys lessons."

Albert sits down next to me and smiles, but the shadows play around his face and his lips curl in a sinister way. The threats are very real when he speaks. "Sounds like fun. Have they heard of cricket?"

I shrug my stiff shoulders. "Maybe, but they don't have funds for a cricket team."

"Pity," he says. "Swinging a bat can build up all sorts of muscles. Great team sport. Character building."

I smile and the words slip out before I realize I didn't just say them in my head. "I take it you don't play cricket then, sir?"

It's difficult to maintain my amicable expression while he gapes at me, but I manage. A sharp jolt runs through me; I think it's thrill. I'm not sure where my audacity came from, but I need to keep it with me.

"Ah." He looks around, fiddles a little with the ostentatious cuffs on his shirt and turns to me. This time his eyes are harder than I've ever seen them, and I wonder if showing him that level of intelligence this early was a mistake. "You should come and watch me play cricket. We have a booth in the stands. I've hit more than my fair share of sixes."

"I'll have to check our schedule." Ice wells inside me, scared because I know how hard cricket balls are. I shouldn't have goaded him, not yet.

"Excellent," he says, and turns to my father to make light conversation, or charm him, or reinforce whatever witchcraft he uses to keep our parents in line.

Suddenly released from his intensity, I push my food around my plate. I'm sure it's as good as everything Joan makes, yet I can't find an appetite.

"Not hungry?" Albert's voice is inches from my ear, and I stiffen momentarily, unsure of how to react.

I turn abruptly to look directly at him, his eyes far too close for my comfort, and the sudden understanding freezes me in my place. As if he understands my expression, he leans in slightly. His hand touches my side ever so briefly, but enough to make it feel like a thousand ants are swarming over my skin trying to devour me like the dying insects on the pavement.

And right now, there's nothing I can do about it.

INTERROGATION

$\mathcal{A}$s soon as I step out of the Causeway kitchen the following morning, Thomas's gaze follows me everywhere. When I settle to go over some letters questions the boys have. When I finally sit down to give them a short tale before they run off to lunch. Even when I'm telling the tale while I watch for signs of any new recruits to the thieving gangs.

Once I'm done though, it's suddenly chill in the air, and I look around to find that Thomas is gone. The bottom drops out from under me, and for a few moments as I look down my feet are dangling in the night sky over the roofs of London while the wind gently chafes my lips and everyone—including Thomas—flies toward the star without me as I begin to plummet—

"Wendy?"

I blink and am back in the chair, grounded, with Thomas at my elbow. Here. Not there. Not gone.

But I can't look him in the eye, not quite yet while I'm still catching my breath, getting my bearings.

"Boys," I say, clapping my hands together and motioning for them to gather around. "I want you to think of the most fun thing you would want to do with Neverland. I'll hear all of your answers tomorrow morning. You don't have to do it alone. Get into groups, act it out. Let's have fun!"

They smile and laugh, and I miss Tybalt again. He always led, would always ask questions, and never, ever let me leave early. I wish I could fetch him, but once you become a lost boy, you can never return. That's part of the deal, and I understand why now.

"Wendy, we need to talk." Thomas's hushed tones have an edge to them I've not heard before, and I look up, suddenly afraid.

"What's wrong?"

"They've..." And he falls silent as Mrs. Johnson approaches, two constables in her wake.

To me, it's immediately clear why they're here, and my mind races to compensate as I fix a suitable smile to my face while they approach.

"Wendy." Mrs. Johnson's expression is relieved, and she smiles tentatively in my direction. "Do you think you can spare a few moments for these constables?"

She gestures at the two uniformed men.

"Of course. Mother won't mind if I'm a little tardy." Smile still affixed to my face, I smooth my expression as best I can while one of the men steps forward.

"Miss, I'm Constable Dapner. We'd like to ask you some questions if that's all right?" the first asks me.

I incline my head. "Of course, constable."

I hope the words don't come out as shaky as I feel.

"Mrs. Johnson 'ere is a bit worried. Three of her boys have gone missin' this last month, an' we're just trying to be clear on who they may have interacted with, or who might've seen them walkin' off with someone."

"Sometimes they misbehave and are sent to one of the solitary bedrooms in the cellar. They're not there, are they?" I didn't realize my mouth could say so much without my willing it to, and I truly hope my face is reflecting concern right now, because I need time to recover.

The constables look at each other briefly, and Mrs. Johnson has gone pale. As if she's surprised I know about the boy's punishment area and she'd prefer to forget it exists. They both look at her, and my stomach flips a bit at having ratted her out.

She rallies, though, and smiles faintly. "No, we checked. They're definitely nowhere on the premises."

I nod, as if I expected that answer all along and continue my response. "I teach letters to all of the boys. I read to them almost every day. So I do interact with them quite frequently."

"The boys were James, David, and Tybalt." Officer Dapner flicks through a small notebook that slots into the palm of his hand. It would be far larger in mine, and for a moment he reminds me of a large bear.

"I know of all of them. They all love story time." I bring my voice down a notch, and make sure my voice catches on the last word. "Are they really all...gone?"

Mrs. Johnson rubs a stray tear from her eye, and I notice the worry lines around her eyes and mouth have increased. She looks suddenly so much older, and the grey in her hair as it sneaks out of her bun cover is suddenly stark against the remaining dark. I'm torn for a moment.

Guilt wrenches at my stomach as she speaks. "Yes."

"Could they—" I continue, in for a penny, in for a pound, "Could they have run away?"

"Of course they could've, miss." Dapner inclines his head, almost as if he's apologizing. "We just have to cover everythin' you understand, right?"

"Of course." The worry I inject into my expression isn't really feigned. We still have three boys at least to help. This much attention isn't good. "Please let me know if I can help in any way."

Suddenly the second man speaks up. "If you think of anything at all, please contact either Constable Dapner, or myself, Constable Baker." His brow constantly shifts through a variety of irritation. He's far sterner than his partner.

"We will." Thomas speaks up for the first time since they entered the room, and both men blink at him. He holds out his hand and shakes each of the constables' before giving them a slight nod of his head.

Mrs. Johnson ushers them out, and we stand there, waiting until we can't hear or see them anymore.

Thomas places a hand briefly on my shoulder to get my attention, and when it leaves its perch, there's a sudden chill where the warmth was but seconds ago. I wait for him to speak whatever is on his mind.

"We need to be careful," he murmurs, so close to my ear. At this distance it feels right, like home, a place I can feel safe to really speak my mind about the things I want.

"I don't think my stories are giving them ideas," I reply, softly. You never know when people are listening, after all. "What we're doing is right, Thomas."

Thomas chuckles. "Yes, ma'am." He says and I turn to face him, mock glare in tow.

"I'm not a ma'am. I'm barely even a miss." I can feel the pout, and even though I try to adjust the expression, I'm irritated, so quite certain it just turns into a scowl.

The look on his face startles me. There's this strange gleam to his eye that I've only seen a few times when he thinks I'm not looking. He reaches out a hand hesitantly and strokes a piece of hair back behind my ear. The touch of his finger as it briefly brushes against my skin sends a shiver down my spine that I don't to stop, even though I know he just broke about a thousand rules of etiquette. But while Thomas makes me want to move closer with his touch, the man my parents want me to marry makes me want to run away. Run away and never return. Would it really be so bad?

"I think you're definitely a miss, Wendy." He grins and winks at me, breaking the spell briefly before it's shattered as the boys all file back out.

I stifle a very unladylike groan as I glance at the clock and realize I'm cutting it horribly close, yet again. Mother is expecting me home for our own lunch. I hope we don't have afternoon plans, because I have to get Joshua to the way-house before dark.

*J*oshua follows me meekly as I lead him along the footpath, and as long as I keep my head bowed under this strangely large hat, I merely look like a lady walking with her son.

"Wendy. Will I get to see the others?" Joshua asks, keeping up banter. He's not as hesitant as Tybalt was. Ty was all talk with other people around, and genuinely shy in my presence. Joshua is astute. He wants to know everything and he wants to know it five minutes ago. He's as curious as I was, as my brothers were, and for a moment I hesitate in taking him to Neverland. He'd probably make a fine grown up.

"Of course you'll get to see the others," I say. "They're there, in Neverland, not a day older than when you saw them last."

He squeezes my hand and begins to pick up the pace, but I pull him back. If we walk too fast, we'll be noticed. After the constables' visit today, we can't afford to be noticed. I'm not sure the excuse of, *but constable, I'm taking them to Neverland where they never have to grow up and get to make their own rules* is going to go over too well with the watch.

Not to mention they may think I'm a little crazy.

I incline my head as a couple with two children pass us. They're busy talking amongst themselves, but it's the odd things we remember most, and an impolite mother with her son is sure to be remembered. Two gentlemen pass us next; their discussion seems heated. Perhaps it's leaking over, because the heat of the sun suddenly feels unbearable. I nod in recognition as they walk past us and notice that Joshua does the same. Good boy. They barely off their own gesture as caught up in their discussion as they are. By the time we make it to the wayhouse, we've passed another lady and her maid, as well as a group of children headed to the church grounds, and I'm a nervous wreck.

One of them might remember us. I'm sure I acted appropriately, but now, even I'm starting to doubt the wisdom of our scheme. We sneak in the back after double and triple checking that no one will see us. I wouldn't be surprised if someone else is inside at this rate.

Joshua crinkles his nose a little when we get to the door. I sniff the air and notice a musty, dirty sort of smell. Those blasted rats and their defecating everywhere. Maybe I'll have to resort to poison. If the stench gets in my clothes again, Mother will start to think something's up.

"What's that smell?" Joshua asks, hesitating as I step over the threshold and hold out my hand to him.

I shrug. "It's musty and old. And sometimes rats scurry around."

I resist the urge to tell him its haunted, after all rumors have been very helpful in maintaining this way-house.

"Really?" His face lights up, and he looks around and steps in after me. "I love me some rats. The Causeway has weird smells too. If you go into the cellar, they're even worse. Old and almost rotten, like someone forgot to empty the food bins in the kitchen. Might be rats in there too?"

"Likely." I think he's nervous. The words pour from his mouth so fast I can barely keep up. Before we head down, I take him by the shoulders and look him in the eyes. "Are you sure you want to go to Neverland? To meet Peter, and see the others? Remember, they won't let you come back."

"But you came back, Wendy."

I shake my head for a moment, and realize he won't understand if I tell him there's only a small part of me that made it back from Neverland. Then I smile, trying to put all the care and feelings I have into it. "I came back because there were too many people here who'd miss me when I'm gone." I end the last very softly, trying not to hurt his feelings too much.

Joshua shrinks back a little and then purses his lips.

"Fine," he says, and the determination leaks into his whole stance, the rigid shoulders, the tall spine. "Let's get on with it."

I take his hand and guide him down the stairs. "I'll make you some tea, and then I have to head home. But I'll be back once the sun is down to introduce Peter to you."

"I have to wait here that long?" He fidgets with his fingers, his hands running through his hair.

"Sorry, Joshua," I say, and for a moment I truly am sorry. "But they can't navigate before twilight sets in. So I'll be back then."

He nods, and I turn to busy myself with the tiny kettle, dropping the leaves in gently as it comes to the boil. I can't stand over it for long or it makes me feel a little lightheaded. But the boiling never takes long once the kindling catches fire.

I pour the tea into a cup and turn to find Joshua swimming in the cushions. Laughter catches me by surprise, and I almost drop the cup, but save it at the last second. "At least I know you won't get too bored while I'm gone."

Joshua grins and takes the cup from my hands. "Well, there are rats too, right? Is this the tea Tinkerbell gave you?" he asks, his eyes shining so eagerly that I'd probably answer yes even if it was a lie.

But I nod, even if that's not quite how it happened, and add for good measure. "That's the tea."

He waits for a few moments, blowing on it to cool it down and gulps a few mouthfuls at once before wiping his free hand across the back of his mouth and grimacing. "Couldn't she have waved a faerie wand and made it taste less..."

"Disgusting?" I reply and pat him on the head.

"Yeah. It's so sweet and somehow bitter...not fun." He downs the rest of it and lays back against the cushions, smiling up at me. "I'll never want anything sweet again."

I laugh at the absurdity and unique accuracy of what he's saying. A young boy never wanting sweets again. The tea works remarkably quickly; I only hope it stays in effect until I manage to make it back.

Joshua blinks up at me, a small smile on his lips. "Thank you, Wendy. I can't wait to get to Neverland."

REALIZATION

Mother doesn't appear to be home when I creep into the house. Joan is humming to herself as I enter the back door to the kitchen. She almost drops a tray, jumping slightly when she realizes I'm there.

"Miss Wendy, you startled me." Her smile is a little forced if the pinch of her brow is anything to go by, and she's probably a little shaken. I feel bad for having shocked her.

"Sorry, Joan. Just wanted to come in quietly. Didn't mean to scare you."

She laughs, and it peals sweetly. "That's aw'right, I'm made of sterner stuff than that. Any snacks you need?" She winks at me, and I remember fondly the times just after she started where she'd sneak me cakes, just after I'd left the nursery.

"Not today, but I'll hold you to that," I say as I leave the kitchen.

I climb the stairs quietly and almost run into Mr. Darby at the top of the steps. The boys' tutor tips his hat to me as he hurries down the way I just came. For a few moments, I watch him go. He's an odd sort of man. Never speaks unless absolutely necessary and always seemed to resent having to teach me. Oh well. I shrug and finally make my way to my room, where I collapse onto my bed after loosening the laces of my dress. If I close my eyes and calm my breathing, I can hear my brothers playing in their room down the hall.

From the noise, I think they're playing pirates and lost boys, jumping from bed to bed and generally having the childhood I miss so much. For a split second I almost sit up, run and grab them, wanting to preserve them forever. But they're not mine to preserve; they're Mother and Father's.

But the boys from Stepney? They belong to no one. They have no one. No one but Thomas, no one but me. We've only moved three of the boys to Neverland—four once Joshua goes tonight—and there are still another two I know of that we have to help. It's a little over-whelming, but I don't have time for dwelling on it.

"Wendy!" John's voice echoes through the upper level of the house, ripping me out of my self-recrimination. There are so many reasons I'm grateful for my siblings, but this is not one of them.

"What?" I call out.

"You have to get us ready for dinner. Mother isn't here, and she said you would." He opens my door and pokes his head around, grin-ning from ear to ear. His face is like a caricature—nose almost too big, eyes round and huge behind the lenses he's had to wear for as long as I can remember. He's tall and gangly, very awkward for his age. I love every inch of him. I'm proud of everything he does. Even interrupting me.

"Go back to the nursery. I'll be there in a moment."

I wait for a few seconds before sitting back up and brushing my skirts down, adjusting my laces. The noise starts again, and I'm quite certain they've gone back to their pirate games and completely forgotten the fact they both need to eat. I wish I was playing with them.

Every time I step into the nursery, I'm hit with so many memories and sensations it's hard to breathe. I'm not sure they know how good they have it or how amazing their childhood actually is.

Why couldn't I be born a boy too? Why can't I have the same options as my brothers? If I really need taking care of, couldn't they just wrap me in a blanket and pop me here, in a corner?

Such a silly thought, and I bend down as Michael runs into my arms and hug him for all he's worth.

"Wendy, Wendy! Can we play a bit?"

I nod to reinforce my words. "Just a little bit. We have to eat, after all. You need the energy."

"But we've got energy, Wendy." John stands tall at the edge of the bed, his toy sword waving high in the air while Michael falls out of my lap and convulses with giggles on the floor.

"Still," I say, trying not to laugh, "if I don't help feed you, I'll get in trouble."

Michael sobers up, pushes himself to standing and hugs me, clinging softly. "No trouble for Wendy. No trouble," he murmurs and I pet him on the head.

Sometimes the feeling of love I have for the two of them threatens to choke me and I hug him back just as tightly.

I have another trip to take tonight to make sure Joshua makes it safely. But I'll make sure the boys are sound asleep first. They are my family.

～

My parents don't get home until I've put the boys to sleep and retreated to my own room. Their obvious attempt at silence as they move around is a level of consideration I appreciate from them, especially since if they think I'm asleep, they'll leave me alone.

For the first time, I'm hesitant to dress myself in one of my hidden smocks. Mother may have thrown the one away, but I have a few left in store. Still though, it might be better for me to wear pants. I clutch the pair of trousers and the jacket I took from John's clothes. Appearing to be a boy is far less conspicuous than a girl wandering around at night. Standing at my bed, hair bound tightly behind me, I smooth my smock down and tuck it into the trousers before pulling over the jacket.

The pants are a little short, and the jacket doesn't quite reach my wrists. I pull a cap over my head and glance in the mirror, unable to recognize myself. With the police already wary, this is a far better disguise. Girls just don't walk around at night.

I look at my bed. My palms sweat as I tuck cushions in as close to a body like resemblance as I can and settle the doll in as my head again. I've had her for as long as I can remember, with her hair the same color as mine and a pretty pale blue dress. It's the hair that I need right now. It'll withstand any perfunctory glance, and I truly hope that after a long day, that's all my mother has time for.

Once I'm happy with it, I creep down the stairs to the kitchen and make sure Joan isn't still here. She's rarely around this time of night, but after scaring her earlier this evening, the last thing I need to do is stumble across her at night if she's chosen to work late. Relieved that she doesn't seem to be around, I close the door softly behind me.

The summer twilight is always so beautiful as we inch out of the season. Red hues light the sky as the sun slips behind the horizon leaving illumination up to the moon. It lights my way, and I'm wary of too many watches. I'm quite certain they've increased their vigilance, and really hope it isn't going to stop us smuggling the rest who need it out of the orphanage.

I double back around, taking a side street every time I even suspect a person in the distance could come my way and approach the house from a different direction, using Belgrave to Durnham instead of White Horse. Even if I'm not as confident on the watch around that area, at least I'm not being too obvious about where I'm going.

The trouser material itches at my calves, and the short boots I'm wearing don't fit quite right. If I'm going to keep this up, I'll have to do better than this haphazard disguise.

Looking each way just in case someone else is out here at this time of night, I then duck into the side path to the rear of the way-house. After the horrid amount of encounters this afternoon, this trip by myself is a relief. The house is in the perfect location, near a church so no one really notices it, with a lot of rumors surrounding it—which means no one really wants to buy it. Superstitious lot.

Pushing through the door, I walk purposefully to the cellar, the blood-red of the sunset still lingering in the sky and bleeding through the windows to lend an eerie appearance to the great hall as I pass through it. A candle is burning in the cellar, so it's the first time I've come back at night recently to a lit room. It's much nicer than trying to gauge the steps in the pitch black.

I'm almost to the bottom when the smell hits me. It's like a rolling cloud of stench that almost knocks me to my knees, except I'm coming down the steps and so I plant myself unceremoniously on one of them to recover. As quickly as it came, it's gone, and it leaves me to wonder if the sewer system is old and has rotted through in this house. Or if it's those pesky rats. Did I ever get around to laying the poison I found in the kitchen cupboard down? I shake my head, unsure. There's been so much going on lately.

The stench probably doesn't lend itself to the house selling. And while up until now that's worked in my favor, I'm not too sure if I can handle spending more time here when that smell will permeate everything I wear and make me retch up any of the food I've eaten.

I wave at Joshua who's lying on the cushions, half smiling in the calm the tea allows him to feel. I go about my business, tidying up a little and waiting for Peter to come and pick up his latest charge.

"It'll be fun, Joshua." I find myself speaking before I realize the thoughts have made their way out, and it doesn't hurt to continue.

He has to be feeling nervous. In fact, as I look at him, his skin has that pallor to it, the pale you get only when you're kind of scared of something.

"Hey," I say, crouching down and stroking his forehead. It's cool and clammy. I didn't realize just how scared he'd be because he was putting on such a brave face earlier. "It'll be fine, Joshua."

I pat his hair and stand up as I see a light flit through the window. Peter won't be long either.

Joshua just looks at me, as if all the trust he has in the world is mine. It's a lot of pressure, so I'm relieved when Peter finally shows.

"Wendy." He says my name the way no one else does. Like we're in a candy shop and the owner takes out those roasted peanuts and lets me taste them. My name sounds so exotic when Peter lets it roll off his tongue.

"Peter," I answer, knowing I don't have nearly the same effect on him.

"Who's this?" he asks, gesturing to the struggling Joshua. Those damned cushions really weren't the best resting place to provide to people.

"This is Joshua. They've been using him in the thieving ring, just like the others. Take him with you?" I ask the question looking directly in Peter's eye, and he does that cap tip, and sly little wink I'm finding myself more and more repulsed by.

"Your wish, my dear Wendy," he says, in that molten voice. It's the only power he still has over me, I swear.

"Just please, Peter. Make sure he gets to the lost boys. Make sure they get their eternal childhood?" I whisper it softly, not wanting Joshua to hear. I have this strange feeling that something isn't right, and I don't know how to make it better. Perhaps Neverland is in turmoil. Maybe Peter is neglecting to say something. Either way, I just want to be sure they're getting what I've promised them.

Peter nods, face suddenly somber. "I promise they'll never have to grow up, Wendy."

Even though the sound of my name uttered by him is still amazing, it rolls off my back. He's fun, and he's cheeky, independent, and stubborn. But if I wasn't bringing these kids here, he wouldn't be going out of his way to try and make sure they got a fighting chance in Neverland or otherwise.

The realization hits me like a punch to the stomach. Peter, despite all the fun we had with him when we visited, despite having the worlds at his fingertips and magic to do anything he wants to for anyone anywhere, is selfish. He never does anything without there being something he wants in it. I'm not sure why he's helping me, but I won't question this gift horse. Not yet.

For the first time since meeting Peter, I'm wary of him.

STAND

I can't afford to fall asleep at the way-house, can't afford to be home late and suffer Mother's wrath for lack of sleep, and can't afford for her to find me dressed in a compilation of John's clothes and my smoke with the remnants of that basement smell still clinging to the fabric. So this time, after they leave, I exit the house immediately and head back toward home.

I'm not sure how I don't wake the entire household when I arrive, but I strip down to my slip in the laundry next to the kitchen and drop my smock and John's clothes into the hamper there. Joan will wash it in the morning, and Mother will never know. I'm certain no one but Nanna saw me in my slip.

The morning dawns far too early, and I grudgingly pull myself out of bed and don a simple but pretty empress line day dress. Mother seems to be obliging my tastes.

I splash my face with the fresh water in my basin. It's amazing how it rejuvenates the will to stay awake. Before I moved out of the nursery, I never needed this extra energy, but then again, before I moved out of the nursery I wasn't gallivanting around for half the night trying to save children and sending them to Neverland.

Mother pops her head around the door just as I finish. "It's almost

"

breakfast time, Wendy. Make sure you're on time. Your father and I have some things we need to discuss with you."

A cold ball of tension nestles itself into my abdomen, and my hunger flees.

The breakfast table looks just as inviting as every morning, but I swear there's a cold front moving into the room as I walk in there, tingeing everything in strange cold hues of grey, pale blue, black, and white. Between one moment and the next I see a memory I'd long not thought of. I remember sitting on Father's knee when John was just a baby and reaching for the jam while the butter on dripped off my bread and onto my Sunday best skirt. Mother scolded me, but Father held me close and hugged me and told her not to mind. I was just a child.

Just a child.

It seems so distant now.

Spread out on the table are trays of sausages and eggs, toast and rolls, butter and preserves, tea and the horrible smelling coffee that my parents only use on special occasions. The ball freezes over.

"Wendy," my father says and pats the spot at the table next to him. "Feels like we haven't spoken in forever."

His smile is just as I remember it, but the lines around his mouth have multiplied, and his eyes look tired. The dark hair I've always been so jealous of has a peppering of silver throughout. I wonder how I missed that Father is aging.

"I'm always here, Father." And I hold my breath, because that's not what I should have said. I don't normally think so little about what I say. But he smiles at me, and I refuse to let the scowl I know Mother is wearing intimidate me when Father isn't offended.

"I know, dear Wendy. I wish I had more time, but work keeps me very busy." He pats the table once more, and I take a seat next to him and reach for some sausage and scrambled eggs. Though I might not be hungry, at least this will distract me.

"Albert will officially begin calling on you in a few days." Father covers my hand with his own, as if he's congratulating me.

I can only hope my mouth isn't hanging open like I think it is.

Calling on me? I blink, trying to gather my thoughts. This is all happening too fast. I thought I had time for this, to plan, to figure out a way out of it without hurting anyone in my family.

Mother is motioning to Father, and if this whole scenario wasn't so dire, it'd be comical. Finally, he lets out a sigh and squeezes my hand. "Your mother doesn't think you should spend so much time at the Causeway now."

I blink at him.

"Why?" I hear myself asking before I can clamp down on my brain.

Father sits back, looking quickly at Mother. I get the feeling he doesn't see the need to confine me like this.

"Wendy, you'll be betrothed soon." The word seems difficult for Father to say, and for a split second I hope that he doesn't really want to marry off his only daughter, but the hesitation is ever so brief, and he carries on. "It's really not becoming of a betrothed lady to be spending so much time with so many boys."

What do they want me to do? Sit at home and knit something? Or paint? Or cross-stitch? I'm not only hopeless at all those things, but Stepney gives me a sense of purpose. Isn't that important? Before I can second guess myself, I stand up and push myself as straight and tall as I can. "I'm sorry, Father, Mother, but I do not believe that is the best thing for me. I love helping people. I'm learning so much by under-standing how to teach the boys, helping prepare meals for them, encouraging them to believe in themselves."

Just as my mother is about to speak, I turn to her and cut her off. "Didn't you tell me that the mark of a good woman, indeed a good wife, is someone who gives of their time, of themselves and what they've learned, and uses it for good?" She looks at me, mouth open a little, as if she can't get the words out, and finally she nods at me. I refuse to stop now, refuse to listen to the shaking my body is doing as I keep up the pace.

"How can I give more than helping at Stepney Causeway? Those boys have nothing. All but a handful are far younger than I, and those that aren't are there as mentors for the younger more than anything. And I'm in the good building, safe with Mrs. Johnson." I stand, breathing in, gathering myself from the words that tumbled out faster than I ever thought I could speak. "I want to be good. I want to help others. I want to help make their lives better."

I fall down more than I sit, but refuse to let my parents see how weak I feel as I hide behind my big words. Mother watches me, a strange new glint in her eye. I hope it means something good. Father waits for a few moments as the grin spreads on his face and finally, he stands up, walks the two steps to my chair and envelops me in a large hug like I haven't had since I was tiny.

He pulls back and looks at me, tucks a strand of hair behind my ear and kisses my cheek.

"My dear Wendy," he says, pride staining his very countenance. "I don't think you realize how proud I am of you in this moment. You're truly the person I always wanted you to be."

I smile, and want to cling to his arms, scream at him that if he loves me so much why is he handing me off to the first available suitor regardless of how I feel about it? But I don't, because I that battle has to wait until I have a real plan of action. "Does this mean I can still volunteer?"

This time Mother speaks, and where I was expecting her to rail against me, it seems my little speech invoked pride in her as well. "Maybe not every day, but definitely a few times a week will still be perfectly fine."

"Thank you." I smile at her, at them both, and I stare at the food on my plate for a moment. The fat of the sausages has congealed around their base, and my stomach churns with the opposite of hunger.

~

My lengthy speech with my parents makes me late for my story session with the boys. I've been far too lenient on them recently, telling them tales of Neverland. I dump the bread basket on the kitchen island and take off my hat, hanging it on my peg on the wall.

"I'm so sorry, Mrs. Johnson. I had things to take care of this morning." My voice sounds foreign to me, as if I've grown over night into this person I no longer recognize and am not sure I want to.

She pats me on the back. "You aw'ways 'ave a good reason when you're late, Wendy. Now hurry through to the boys. I think they began to fear ye wouldn't make it here today at all."

I smile at her but hesitate for a moment. She should know, shouldn't she?

"I won't be able to come every day anymore. Circumstances won't let me." I hope she can hear the sadness in my voice; it's surely there just as it hangs heavy around my heart. "Maybe three days a week."

For a moment Mrs. Johnson's lips draw into a thin line, but then she pats me on the shoulder and smiles. "Three days a week is an amazing thing. Anything is more than they had before."

Relieved, I squeeze her hand and head into the room.

"Wendy!" The cry goes up in unison, and I fight back the heat behind my eyes.

This isn't a time for tears; it's a time for learning. And then for talking to Thomas and figuring out our next move.

"Good morning," I say to them, and am surprised to hear the chorus back to me.

"Good morning, Wendy!" they almost shout. Exuberance colors their cheeks, and their eyes shine with enthusiasm. Would that everyone felt such a zest for life.

"Peter Pan!" A voice cries out, and a giggle erupts around the room.

Scanning the crowd, I'm quite certain the speaker was Stephen, growing a little more boisterous now that Tybalt has been gone some days. A flurry of butterflies upsets my stomach as I realize they'll both be together again soon.

I shake my head. Not only did the name elicit a strange feeling in my stomach for the first time ever, but really, I can't just tell stories. They'll never have the skills they need to make it if I can't get them to Neverland, and then that'll be my fault. "We can't always tell stories. Today we need to practice letters."

Groaning echoes around the room as Thomas gets out the slates. He knows the drill, and I notice he takes one for himself. The younger ones practice their names and then their numbers. Just writing them out and getting used to the feel of it. Older ones do some simple math and words. I'm no teacher, but I've always loved sitting in with the boys as they learned such rudimentary things. Michael can almost write his own name now, and John is adept at calculating almost anything in his head.

Time flies just as quickly this way, and some of the boys seem shocked to hear the lunch bell ring for the first round of eaters. The slate clicks together in a way that reminds me of a drum beat. The bow of the ship heaves under my feet as I recall the pirate ship and war drums, the lost boys and their parties—

"Wendy?"

I blink up to realize Thomas is standing next to me, and the flush of my cheeks is hot as I notice his hand resting on my shoulder. I'm almost betrothed, shouldn't I tell him to remove his hand? What if I don't want to? Does that mean there's something wrong with me?

"Did everything go all right?" His voice is hushed, and his eyes dart here and there making sure no one can overhear us.

I nod. "Perfectly. Slipped off to Neverland like he was falling into a dream."

Thomas smiles, and for a moment I think he's about to ask me, to request that I take him with me next time and stay with him there. Sometimes I think I see it in his eyes, however fleetingly. Maybe it's just wishful thinking on my behalf.

"When can we take Henry?"

I blink at him. "Maybe we should take Henry before it becomes too noticeable that Joshua is gone?" It makes sense not to have the watch even more alert than they are right now. After all, the more patrols, the more the public is aware of runaway boys, the more they'll notice boys walking around.

"Tomorrow night?" he asks, and I ponder it for a moment before he speaks again. "If you walk them to the way-house, it won't be a boy on his own. Which is what they're looking for. Boys, running away from things by themselves."

He focuses on me intently, a little sad and contemplative.

Sometimes I think Thomas is a little too emotional for all of this. Not just getting the boys to safety, but being here, in this orphanage. Yet I've never had enough courage to ask him why he's here, why he hasn't found a home. I don't suppose any of them really know.

I smile and squeeze his arm briefly as I stand up. The feel of his skin is soft and warm beneath my fingers, and I want to let my hand linger where I know it shouldn't. Am I just rebelling against my parents' plans? Is my heart beating so fast for him or for my being so daring to contemplate things I shouldn't?

"Tomorrow night it is, then," I say, distracting myself from my own thoughts and conflicting emotions.

Thomas smiles and leaves the room to go and eat. Standing in front of my chair I suddenly feel very, very alone.

LURKING

*L*oud pounding on my door is the last thing I expect on a Saturday morning. I blink through sleep filled eyes in its direction, hoping to make it spontaneously combust. On second thoughts it might be one of my brothers, so instead, I croak out. "Just a moment."

As I push myself upright, the room spins, and I have to count to five before trying to move. I didn't sleep enough. Again. But then, I wasn't expecting to be woken up this early on a Saturday. I thought I had plenty of time to sleep and recover from helping Henry cross over to Neverland last night.

Gingerly, I place a foot on the ground and stand, gripping onto my bed frame. The world tilts a little, but rights itself relatively quickly and I let out a pent-up sigh of relief. I grab my dressing gown from the front of my dresser and wrap it around as best I can before opening the door.

John stands there, fist raised to knock again, but a huge smile spreads over his face as he sees me.

"Mother isn't going to be happy." He says it in a teasing tone, but I'm quite certain there's some truth to it.

"What have I done now?" I ask, resigned to the fact that it's probably something very major.

But my brother shakes his head and grins. "You haven't done anything. Except not been awake and dressed yet."

"John, please just tell me. I'm very tired."

He peers in my room, or tries his very best to look past me. "What did you do so late that you'd be tired? I thought you went to bed just after we did last night?"

I shrug. "Had trouble sleeping."

It's not exactly a lie. It's definitely difficult to sleep while you walk through the city.

"Well," He glances down the stairs, gesturing wildly with his right hand. "You have a visitor! Mother told me to tell you to get dressed and Joan is bringing clean water for you to wash down with."

A visitor? My knees shake a bit, because there's only one visitor Mother would make me hurry to greet. It can't be him, can it? What sort of person doesn't announce their coming earlier? Or maybe he did, and Mother didn't tell me.

Without really thinking about it, I close the door in John's face only briefly seeing his indignation before it swings shut. There's no time for that now. As I make my way to the closet, it feels like I'm floating above myself, watching my every action, going through the motions. It's an eerie sensation and I don't like it.

At all.

The knock at the door sounds distant, echoes through my head like drops of water in an empty sink.

"Come in." I hear myself say, though I don't even remember thinking it. "Thanks, Joan," I mutter, as she places the new bowl, exchanging it for the old, and wipes my jug out and down.

"Miss Wendy?"

I turn, blinking at her, wondering when it got so bright in my room and why everything is blurry. Something wet rolls down my cheek and plops onto my shoulder and I wipe it away without thinking, only to realize it's a tear. Strange, I don't remember crying.

"Yes?" I ask her as my voice catches, and the tears suddenly seem so much more real and necessary.

"Can I do anything for you?"

"For me?" And for a fleeting moment I wonder if she'd chase Albert away. Tell him I have a headache or I've run away. But then I realize I'm in panic mode, and that's most definitely not what she meant by the question at all.

So, I smile at her and nod my head. "I probably need some help with my hair, and whichever dress I should wear. Must be quick, right?"

Even though I ask the latter more of myself than of Joan, she obliges me with an answer.

"Faster would be better, miss." And she moves to dutifully go through my closet while I rinse cloths in fresh water and wipe myself down. Tonight, I really want to have a long bath. I can feel the grime of the way-house on my skin regardless of how hard I rub. With Albert waiting downstairs, I don't want a trace of the smell mother noticed, but red raw skin also isn't appropriate.

I turn back toward Joan, and I'm not sure how much time passed, but she has my underskirts ready, shoes and stockings picked out and a lovely dress I swear I didn't even realize I owned. Or I may not have owned it until recently and therefore not have realized it. Mother can be sneaky like that. Mother can be sneaky all the time.

A pale, almost apricot sheer fabric hangs over a calico underskirt. The top layer has strategically placed roses situated on it with tiny puffs of embroidered flowers all over the rest of it. It's light and airy, summery and young at heart. It calls out to me in a way clothing is starting to do with scary frequency.

Tentatively, I reach out my hand with a glance to Joan.

"Is this new?" I ask her, almost afraid to touch it.

Joan nods. She smiles. "Your mother 'ad it made new."

For a few moments I wonder if I should wear it, if I should give Mother that amount of satisfaction. I know I should, even if I don't want to.

"Excellent." I smile, determined to make the best out of it while I still have to.

Undergarments on, dress arranged, I stand in front of the mirror while Joan hurriedly sees to my hair. The peach-like accents highlight my face and make me look far older than I feel.

Finally, Joan finishes and I drink in my countenance for a little while. It's hard to see this reflection, the one that doesn't look like the me who first flew to Neverland at all. The one who looks like a smaller version of Mother—like I'm about to be an adult. Chills fight down my spine for dominance. In the end there's room for all of them.

I tear my gaze away from the mirror.

"Thank you, Joan." I know she did an amazing job with very little time. She does a tiny curtsy and hurries from the room.

I'm about as ready as never to face what's downstairs. Time to get this over with.

When I reach the bottom of the stairs, Mother is waiting for me. She looks me up and down and has me turn around once. "You look presentable, if a little tired."

"It's Saturday," I say in my defense and resist the urge to roll my eyes at her. "I slept badly."

She sighs and turns around. "Follow me."

As we approach the dining room, thoughts start to battle in my head. Can I decline his advances? Am I allowed to say no if he does ask for my hand, or do I fall out of the negotiations? I don't want to end up as a Mrs. Davenport.

"Wendy." Albert's tone is warm and inviting, as if he's been looking forward to seeing me for a very long time. His charm is off-putting and insincere, and I'm quite sure he knows it.

"Albert," I reply, inclining my head politely, but I refuse to say anything else. It may be rude, but it's the only way I can rebel right now.

He grins at me, and takes my hand, laying a kiss on it and I remove it from his grasp immediately. "I hope you'll forgive my calling early, but I was hoping we might enjoy a day out together. Reminisce about our childhood days."

"Of course," I reply, wondering if Mother can tell my teeth are clenched. "Where were you thinking?"

Albert smiles with that same soul-sucking darkness, even if everyone else thinks it's genial. "I have my father's vehicle with me today. Have you ridden in one of the horseless carriages before? They call them cars."

He offers his hand, which I ignore, grinning expectantly. There's a strange gleam behind his expression that I can't place, but I have no illusions about how much fun the day will be.

I shake my head, mostly because I don't want to go, but also because I've not ridden in one of those contraptions yet. "I've never been in one. Where did you think to go?"

Maybe if my parents know where I'm going he can't leave me behind.

He smiles and hooks my arm through his. I want to push him off, but I smile instead and he answers my question. "Kensington Gardens."

I try to suppress the gasp, but some of it still escapes me and he laughs. "It's not as far as you might think when you're riding in a car."

With one last desperate—and ignored—glance in my mother's direction, I nod. "Shall we, then?"

He almost drags me out of the house, and I notice that beneath that wiry and tall frame, he has more strength than I realized. His grip is tight as he leads me to the vehicle and helps me step into it. The seats are a little hard and uncomfortable, and when he starts the strange thing, it's quite loud. Much louder than the melodic clip-clop of a horse's feet. All I can think of is how much I truly do not want to be here.

ensington Gardens would be beautiful, if not for the fact that Albert won't let me go. It's worse than that day at my house, but he grips my upper arm, or my forearm as if scared I'll jump out of his moving car. Not that it would be difficult to fall out considering how bumpy a ride it is. I'm not sure what he eats, but it's like his bones are made out of steel. Half way through our trip and I'm sure I already see bruising starting to appear.

"You haven't changed a bit." I whisper, still trying to wrench my arm out of his grip.

He stops, and the grip loosens. "Wendy. Wendy. Even back then I knew they had plans for us. It's why they threw us together so often. No one believed your stories then, and no one will listen now. You're fifteen next week. Please stop spinning the tales."

The anger seeps in through his touch, fueling the fire that's been smoldering since my parents told me of this silly plan. "They'll believe me. Don't you worry. I'll make sure everyone knows."

The words sound foolish the moment they leave my lips, but strength suffuses me and I know I won't take this lying down.

Until he pushes me against the next tree we walk past, and its bark digs into my back.

"Really?" His breath stinks of tea and spite. "That's not how this works. Your mother wants this for you. And my father wants this so he can give more to *your* father."

Is he threatening my father? I gulp, refusing to look away from his eyes. "You can't."

"I can't?" For a moment he almost wins me over with the confusion on his face, but the expression hardens and he lets go of me, turning around hands on his hips. "This isn't ideal for either of us, but it's better for you."

I shake my head. "You don't make any sense. We've always disliked each other. Why would you even want to go through with this?"

He has to have some logic in that thick head of his, doesn't he?

He turns around once more, facing me, and takes two steps in my direction. I back up against the tree, ignoring the dig of bark in my back. My heart beats faster, and even I can smell my own fear as he leans forward and breathes the next words into my ear.

"I want this because my mother wants her friend to be happy. Despite what you think, I do love my mother. You will get everything you need. All the care, all the help. You just need to understand that they're all trying to do you a favor." He steps back and won't meet my eyes as he waits for me to gather myself.

The heat that rushes to my cheeks has nothing to do with his words, or my own intimidation, but far more with embarrassment that someone might have seen how closely he stood to me. So many names run through my head to call him, not one of them nice or Albert. I glower at him as he forcefully joins our elbows again and run through every possible solution in my mind. There has to be something I can do.

The ride back to my parent's house is blessedly silent, of speech at least, not the car's engine, which is what I think he called the thing that runs it. The sun is beginning to set as we pull up to my street, and my stomach aches with the lack of food I've eaten all day. No breakfast, because I was dragged out of the house, a tiny lunch, and so far, no dinner. I'll be lucky if I can sneak some supper. I wonder if I could smack Albert over the head and ask Peter to drop him in the Neversea.

I'm surprised when Albert pulls past our house a ways and wonder if he forgot momentarily where I live.

"I'll walk back." I say.

Just as I go to get out of the car though, he places his hand in front of me, stopping me.

"Not quite yet. We need to talk." That gleam is back in his eye. He leans in close, his breath slides over my skin as he speaks. "You're lucky to be marrying me. You're lucky I understand the other options."

He says the words, leaning in toward my neck.

I freeze, for a moment before speaking as evenly as I can. "Get away from me, Albert."

He leans back a moment, and I think I see frustration in his eyes. "You shouldn't be scared of me, Wendy."

My heart beats in my chest and I want to push him away and run screaming, but I'm paralyzed. I'm not scared, I'm terrified. It takes every ounce of energy I have to nod my head, because in these close quarters, I am scared.

"Good." He whispers again, reaching past me to push open the door. "Don't forget that."

ALONE

My dash through the kitchen avoids my parents and I race up the stairs, almost subconsciously skipping that sixth step. I don't want anyone to know I'm home, to see me before I can look at myself. Those few seconds before I reach my room move agonizingly slowly, as if some force doesn't want me to make it. Of course, that's complete nonsense, and my bedroom door clicks behind me with a finality that echoes in my bones, locking me in this situation, threatening never to let me out.

A few of his fingerprints are already darkening into bruises as I peel down this dress. It was so pretty this morning yet seems so ugly now. I steel myself and look in the mirror. When did I start looking like a lost girl? The forlorn and waifish appearance startles me. I didn't realize I'd lost weight, or that my lack of sleep was getting to me. My expression and face is pinched, tired, and wan, while the shine to my hair has grown dull. And the truth is, I think I feel every inch as bad as I look.

My reflection is not of the me I want to be, but the me I may be forced to become.

A tear snakes its way down my face, and I splay my fingers against the mirror as I watch it trickle down. Even my eyes seem dull, lifeless.

There's a knock on my door, and I blink the tear away hurriedly, pulling the top back up to cover the bruising that is beginning to appear and forget that I must have scraped my back against the tree. Albert is a bully. I just need a way to fight back.

Mother pushes into the room a moment later, the crease between her eyebrows, and a slight scowl that tilts the corner of her mouth. In the blink of an eye she crosses to me and leaves a resounding slap against the pale skin of my left cheek.

My neck and face snap around, so surprised am I by the attack. I lift my hand to touch my cheek even as I feel each individual finger-print standing in growing welts. The tears that pour from my eyes can't be controlled this time, nor can they be blinked away. As I cradle my cheek, I forget to hold the top of my gown over the slip, and it falls, revealing the bruises in perfect round finger-tip size as they form nice purple dots beneath my skin.

Mother gulps visibly. Her mouth works for a moment, the angry line gone from her face, and no sound comes out. I look away.

"Oh, no. Wendy," Her voice tells me she's forcing herself to be calm. "I was worried. You didn't tell us you were home. You didn't even bring Albert inside."

I glance out the window and feel a twinge of guilt. It's almost dark. I didn't realize I'd been standing in here for so long. It's like she can't see the bruises. Ignorance is bliss?

"Sorry. Time—" Neverland. I want to go to Neverland so badly. "I didn't—"

But I'm still crying, and she approaches as if fearful I'll dart away, and very gently gathers me to her, sitting us both on the bed.

"Wendy. My poor Wendy. This is so hard for you."

Her arms are warm and her breath against my hair is soothing. It reminds me of the nights I slept so badly, scared of the boogeyman outside the window. On those nights she would hear me scream and come in to hold me tightly, swaying with me and humming to me under her breath. I just want to bury my head like I did then and never come out, but I can feel her waiting for some sort of explanation. Only I don't know how to form the words.

"I can't do this, Mother." I'm sobbing now, great, heaving gulps I didn't know I was capable of, and she still holds me, murmuring *shhh* and petting my head the whole time. Finally, I think it's all out, and I pull back, dabbing at eyes I know must now be swollen.

"I'm so sorry, Wendy." She sits back from me, and sadness creases her brow, just like the frown that mars her pretty face, but I can also see her calm returning, her grip on reality and any sympathy taking a back seat to what she feels must be done.

"You're not going to put a stop to it, are you? You or Father?" Even though I pose it as a question, I already know the answer, as does the numb concoction of limbs my body has become.

She shakes her head, and bites her lip. I think I do that sometimes. "It's set, Wendy. We accepted on your behalf weeks ago."

She speaks so softly, I have to strain to hear her.

"What gives you the right—I can leave. I can support myself. You don't need to provide for me any longer." The rage is blocking out my desperation, big black dots over my vision. "You can't decide my future for me."

But Mother shakes her head. "We already have, dear. It's done. This is the best thing for you. It's what you need in life."

She's not even a convincing liar. At least I know who I get it from.

"You raised me to be a punching bag?" The silence that greets my question is deafening.

She swallows visibly before answering. Maybe she counts to ten. "No, but—"

"But it's my duty? I didn't ask to be born, Mother. You did that. I didn't ask that you keep me, and you are so fond of reminding me that you and Father had to budget strictly to have us at all. You chose to raise me. If you did it with a thought to having me owe you something, then I think I misunderstand parenthood."

And even as I speak and see her face closing off, I know I've hit a sore spot. One that will dash any chance of her coming to my rescue, but since that chance was always non-existent, I don't feel as if I've lost anything.

Mother stands up and brushes off her skirts. "What's done is done,

Wendy. Don't go spreading baseless rumors. Hold your head high, and remember your family loves you." She moves toward the door, but pauses and looks back. I can see the emotion fighting to get through her facade. Her hesitation is apparent as she steps back toward me. "Do you at least like the dress?"

My glare stops her at arms-length and I demonstrably rip the dress off, quite certain I hear a tear of fabric.

"I hate this dress. Throw it away," I say, stepping out of it and turning my back to avoid looking at her even though I hear her sharp intake of breath.

The door closes as she leaves the room, and for the first time in a long time I feel at peace with my life. Neverland is the only option. For all of us.

~

The next day is Sunday, and it dawns with painful clarity for me. I want to see Thomas, talk to Thomas, feel that overriding peace that he instills in me. But he's not family, and Sundays are supposed to be family time. Glancing in the mirror as I hurry to get dressed, I ignore the ripped dress still strewn across the floor in favor of the reflection that looks back at me. Hollows are forming under my eyes, from the lack of sleep no doubt. My skin is about two shades paler than usual, and I'm normally quite fair. I'd be willing to bet it's a trick mirror if I didn't know otherwise.

Today I shall spend with my brothers, because they're my world right now, when Thomas isn't around. They ground me and refresh the reasons we returned here so I don't go crazy. I need something to look forward to, so I don't give in and go meekly along with the plan.

I smooth down the simple blue dress again and walk toward the door, only to see it begin to open. Maybe it's Mother coming to apologize? I hope not; I'm not ready, and I'm also not that naïve.

"What is..." but my words die on my lips as I see Michael trying his best to juggle a huge plate of food and his teddy bear. His tongue is shoved out of the corner of his mouth as he concentrates on the task ahead of him with amazing focus.

"Why thank you, kind sir." I say, and usher him in with me, relieving him of the tray that's almost as big as he is, and set it on the small table next to my window.

He's soft and squishy and even more fun to snuggle than that teddy bear he drags everywhere. Setting him down, I raise a piece of toast to my mouth, suddenly ravenous.

"Wendy. Is it true?" Michael asks after several minutes of watching me eat.

"Is what true?" I ask, almost spitting egg over him before I can swallow it. Have my parents already told my brothers?

"Are you leaving us?" His voice is soft, and I cringe to hear the fear in it.

I want to reassure him and say no, I'll always be here. But right now I can't promise that. Not with the way things are in our part of the world, in our part of society. If I could only change things, make my own decisions then I'd not have to do this to either of them, to anyone.

"I'll always be near, just not always down the hall," I reply, thinking it the best approach, for now. But tears well up in his eyes and he clings to me.

"What will I do wiffout m-m-my Wendy?" He cries, his little voice hitching on the sobs.

I can feel my heart slowly breaking into a million pieces as I discard what's left of my breakfast and sit him on my knee to rock him against me. He sobs into my chest, dampening the material through to my skin. Yet I don't care. His hands clutch in the fabric as he clings to me in his determination never to leave my side. And I realize how much I don't want him to, how much I don't want to leave him or John.

"I'll always be with you in some way, Michael." I try to soothe him, pet his little head, and hug him tight.

"B-b-buuuut," he wails at me, looking up briefly before burying his head again.

So, I gently pry my dress out of his hands and turn him so he sits on the edge of my knees. I look him straight in those beautiful eyes and try to pour every ounce of caring and love I have for him into my words.

"I'll always be here in one way or another. You'll grow up big and strong, and daring. You'll save people from evil and have lots and lots of friends."

"Really?" he asks me and peers up from under my arm, sobbing halted. "Like Peter Pan?"

"Just like Peter, Michael. Just like Peter." And even as I answer him my stomach grows cold, and I want to warn him to stay away. I want to yell at him, to shake him until he understands that when he's by himself, he needs to stay away from Peter Pan.

DANGER

*M*onday comes so quickly, I feel like someone shortened Sunday and is playing a mean trick on me. At least I managed to avoid Mother most of the day yesterday. This will be my first truncated week at the orphanage, and I can already feel my chest tightening at the thought, even though I'm walking down the street directly to it, clutching the bread basket like it will breathe new life into me.

Each time a car approaches, I cringe momentarily until it continues past me and drives away. Albert isn't anything special, but he thinks he is because he's been allowed to believe that he is. He's worse than Hook.

Mother's lack of compassion for my parent-induced plight scares me. She loves father. I've heard the story often enough. It's far easier to put up with going through many different stages of a life together when you truly care for the other person. I'm only fifteen, and I know that because I could put up with Michael through almost anything. It's a little too warm to be wearing long sleeves today, but I had to cover the bruising that Mother refused to see.

After my outing with Albert, the Causeway buildings don't loom anymore. In fact, they seem almost infantile in comparison. Monsters are everywhere. It's just the way life is. Placing the basket on the table, I unhook my hat and hang it up, realizing belatedly there's already one there.

"Sorry Mrs. Johnson. I'll take them both home today."

"Not to worry dear," she says smiling as she busies herself with the food preparations.

I watch her for a few moments, a frown tugging at my lips. The lady rarely steps foot outside the kitchen. I don't understand how she can be so happy day in and day out in the exact same tasks.

"Wendy."

"Yes, Mrs. Johnson?" I ask, looking up, a little startled.

She bites her lip and stretches her apron out, trying to brush away crumbs or creases, I'm not quite sure. "Could you talk to the boys? Henry is gone now too. I'm not sure if they're all deciding to run away together, or if something went wrong, but you're so good to them."

"I can make sure none of them are too distraught." I don't know how to say no to her without sounding like I'm accusing her of not coming to their aid when she has to know what goes on here. So I try a different approach. "I'm sure they're all fine somewhere."

She watches me for a few moments, and I can see the stress this is causing her as her brows pinch and the worry lines around her mouth deepen. Then I notice all of the silver interspersed in her dark hair again. Maybe my wanting not to grow up leads me to discount how much the adults around me age.

"But we don't know, Wendy. We don't know."

I hesitate for a moment. We do know. I know, but I can't tell her. "True, but we can always hope. Hope helps, doesn't it?"

Mrs. Johnson smiles and reaches over to pat my hand. "Run along. The boys need as much time for lessons as they can get. You're only coming three days a week now, remember?"

I smile and hurry into the boys' room.

"Wendy!"

A few of them chorus my name as I walk through the door.

"Boys!" I grin at them and watch as they practice letters and numbers. "Keep going, I'll come around and see how you're doing."

I drift casually over to where Stephen is concentrating, his tongue sticking out of the side of his mouth and the chalk clutched almost feverishly in his left hand. There's faint bruising left on the skin just inside his collar, as well as several covering his calves easily visible with his shorts. I clench my fists for a moment and count to ten. He's the next one on this list. The last one I'll send to Neverland, for a while anyway.

I scan the whole room and frown. That something off about Peter keeps coming back to haunt me. How he speaks, phrases things, like he knows something I don't. What if I contact Peter, and wait at the house with Stephen and he doesn't come? What do I do if Peter is bored?

Fatigue is my friend this morning, and I fight the constantly drooping eyelids as I watch them, eagerness lighting up their faces. Even in the face of everything else, knowing what they must know about the possibilities that await them, they all find hope, a reason to smile.

Even as I watch, Stephen looks over and grins at me. With a fake salute, he winks and smiles before going back to the simple sums he has on the chalkboard.

"Second thoughts?"

I whirl around to see Thomas standing behind me. And while I knew it was his voice, I'd not seen him there. Instead of annoyed or startled, I feel this pressure release from my chest, and don't even have to think about the smile I can feel spreading.

"Not exactly. I'm trying to figure out how to make things a little bit easier on ourselves." I lean forward and correct young Harold as he draws a three backwards before straightening to continue. "Must be careful now."

Thomas grins and leans in. "But isn't that half the fun?"

I wave him away, trying to fend off a giggle.

"That's not the point." But it sort of is, even just a little bit. I turn toward the boys and clap my hands. "Okay. Let's hear a story, shall we? Of pirates, and treasure, and kidnapping!"

They cheer me on, lending strength to my otherwise somber mood.

~

Usually I'm quite excited—and a little nervous—about the prospect of taking another boy to Neverland. But today's is a little trickier than usual. If the butterflies in my stomach are anything to go by, I think I'm scared.

The home has begun watching the boys more closely, I'll actually have to meet Thomas and Stephen in the park near the Causeway and head over to the way-house once it's already dark.

That also means I need to leave the house as soon as it starts to get dark, preferably slightly earlier. Creeping out of my house during twilight is not the easiest thing in the world. Since the park is close to the orphanage, I try to walk quick and purposefully and all I can think of is how those pillows won't hold up to close inspection. It's all I can do not to run back in panic and creep into bed until the sun is completely down.

What if Michael ventures into my room wanting to hug? And discovers I'm only pillows? He'll need to find me, want to find me. I'll be in so much trouble.

"Breathe, Wendy." I say it out loud hoping to get it out of my system.

The park looms ahead of me, the first leg of this trip almost complete. I truly hope it's my purposeful stride, at least I think that's how I'm walking. It's also not yet dark, and if I hurry, we should make it to Dunstan's church area in time to not raise suspicions either.

I look around the park until Thomas pops out from one of the bushes. Resisting the urge to roll my eyes at him, I kneel down and smile at Stephen. "Are you ready?"

He smiles, and it's a huge and endearing expression. "I can't wait to meet Peter, an' see the others again."

"Let's go." But I don't get further—Thomas catches me by the arm, and I gasp as his fingers close lightly over some of the bruises.

"Wendy? Are you all right?" he asks, concern creasing his brow like an old man.

I snatch my arm away, upset that he's seen my weakness. "I'm fine."

But he grabs me gently by the shoulders and turns me to face him, protocol be damned.

"I don't believe you," he says softly. "Please let me help you."

I look down at the ground, biting my lip, unsure of what to say, of how much I can say. Thomas isn't family; he's not supposed to be involved in things like this. He's my friend, my secret, and I don't want to tarnish him with all these things.

His intake of breath surprises me. "He's hurt you?"

I nod, sniffing back the tears I can feel threatening again. *Wendy! Stop it.*

"Yes." I hear it out loud, and it emboldens me, gives such an inner strength that burns in my chest. "I'll think of something."

"No, *we'll* think of something," he says and pats my shoulder awkwardly.

The heat rises in my cheeks, and I know they must be pink, so I grab Stephen's hand.

"We have to go while it's still light, Thomas. We can talk about other things tomorrow." With a quick smile, I turn on my heel, and Stephen and I walk hand in hand away at a nice controlled pace. If I don't measure out every step, I'll try to run and right now that's probably not the best idea with a young boy in tow when the watch are looking out for young runaways.

The light is fading, and we take the street before White Horse to avoid walking past my family house.

"Will it be safe, Wendy?" Stephen's voice is so tiny, and I can hear the fear, sense it as his sweaty palm grips my hand.

"It'll be safe, and warm, and you'll see everyone again." I squeeze his hand and feel as he grows just a little taller at the sound of my words. Would it were so easy to give myself a boost in confidence, too.

I hear the watch before I see it, and my heart sits in my throat.

"It'll be fun, I swear." I say to Stephen and we approach the cross street the constables are standing on. Their eyes follow our every step, even though their conversation doesn't let up. The one on the left reaches into his pocket, and I'm sure he's about to pull out the whistle and blow it, trying to stop us.

It'll all be over then. Albert will never get me. Maybe it's for the best. My breath is coming fast, in gasps and I try not to let them know that I know they're watching me. Right on cue though, my companion pipes up to answer my question.

"Of course it will be." Stephen laughs softly as he squeezes my hand. "I've been looking forward to this forever."

Out of the corner of my eye, I realize the watch aren't looking our way anymore. The one with his hand in his pockets takes it out and pops something into his mouth. I sigh with relief at the role Stephen didn't even know he was playing. His laugh convinced them he was fine. Lucky for me the fashion is to wear hats. Huge, head-covering hats. Oh, how I hate them, but love their current convenience.

One more little run into a lamplighter. This time Stephen stumbles a little as he turns to crane his neck and watch how the man lights one of the lamps. With the sun almost down, it's no wonder he didn't see the crack, but it's enough for the man to turn and look at us very briefly.

"Silly boy." I murmur to Stephen and he giggles again. "Clumsy."

The man watches us for a moment, shrugs, and carries on, whistling softly something I can't recognize because it's that off-key.

"Sorry," Stephen whispers, grabs my hand and we head on toward the church.

My heart is beating so fast by the time we arrive at the way-house, I think it's going to jump out of my throat. I rest against the door for a few moments, and watch as Stephen crinkles his nose.

"This place smells," he says. "Like something's rotten."

I nod and push us through. Maybe rat poison wasn't the best solution, or maybe the rats are just dying. The sun is at it again as it valiantly tries to cling to the remnants of the day by bathing the main hall in a beautiful red light. So much like blood as we walk through to the cellar.

"It's an old house, Stephen," I say as I guide him carefully down the stairs. Wouldn't want him to fall and break his neck or something. It'd be difficult to explain.

"Does it have mice?" he asks, and I can hear the excitement in his voice.

Boys and rodents. If they keep it up, they'll turn into them.

"Rats. Haven't seen any mice," I say, and watch him at the edge of my vision as his mouth drops open.

"Caww, really? Rats?"

"Huge rats," I answer and laugh at him and light the candles to illuminate the room.

"This is it?" He says and looks around curiously. His expression falls, despite efforts to keep it the same and I can see the disappointment as his shoulders sag and the breath whooshes out of him.

"Silly," I say, "This isn't Neverland. This is just where we wait for Peter."

The immediate smile returns the joy to his eyes and I motion to the cushions to get him to take a seat. "I'll make you some Neverland tea, and we can wait for Peter to arrive."

He sits down and I make a small cup of tea for him, noting that my kindling is going to run out in another few, and my water supply is getting very low. After we sit out a few weeks so the runaway hubbub dies down, I'll have to see to replenishing my supply. Although the tea is still half full. I think I'll have to stop sending boys once it runs out. I wouldn't know how to begin replacing it, these odd leaves and ground berries. I'm not sure I'll remember how to make it again.

"Thanks, Wendy," Stephen says, smiling up at me as I hand him the cup. He smells the liquid and wrinkles his nose, sort of like a rabbit. They all do that. "What is this?"

I blink at him. None of them have asked me that before. It's a plant that brings peace as long as you crush the berries right. "I don't know. It's a tea that relaxes me enough so I can cross over to Neverland if I want to, but I thought to help you all cross over instead."

Stephen takes a sip and cringes. "That's really sweet."

I nod at him, watching as he takes a bigger gulp, and another before setting it on his lap for a moment.

"Don't you want to go to Neverland again, Wendy?" he asks, huge dark eyes looking up at me, searching out my secrets to keep for himself. It's unsettling and the twisting in my stomach extends to my lungs for a second.

Stephen wipes a hand across his eyes as he takes another few gulps to finish off the tea. He's getting tired. They'll probably have to carry him all the way. "Wendy?"

And I realize I've not answered his question. "I always want to go, Stephen. Sometimes there are other things we have to do first."

He smiles at me, and there's a sad tint to his eyes as if he understands what I'm going through when he couldn't possibly.

"You should go with Thomas. Rescue Thomas too, Wendy. If anyone deserves this, he does." Stephen closes his eyes for a few moments, a smile perched on his lips and I watch him, waiting for some more words of wisdom from this ten-year-old.

But he doesn't give them to me, and so I sit, in the damp cellar hoping against hope that Peter hasn't abandoned me, that he'll come and fetch this boy. I need to get home quickly. There's every chance my parents have already discovered my absence and I'm scared of what they might do.

I'm almost dozing myself when I hear a noise and look up. Peter's face is half in shadow, and a trick of the light makes him appear skeleton like. As if he doesn't eat anymore. I've always wondered, if they don't age, do they need to eat?

"I was worried you wouldn't come." I hear the words tumble out and feel a tear on my cheek. It's been so trying these last few times, so draining. All I want to do is go to sleep and dream of the place I'd love to be.

Peter smiles, and suddenly the boy I knew is back. He clicks his heels and winks at me.

"This the boy?" He gestures to where Stephen rests peacefully amongst the cushions, blending with the grey color scheme down here in the shadows of the flickering candle.

"That's him."

Peter sighs. "You make me do all the work, Wendy Darling. Hiding the boys for you, keeping them safe. Now I have to carry them too?"

I grin at him. I'm not sure why or quite when I began thinking bad things about Peter, but he's really quite an amazing person. To do everything for me that he does, is a wonderful thing. "Thank you, Peter."

But as I reach up to kiss him on the cheek before I flee home, I suddenly feel like I'm getting ready to say good-bye.

~

It's late when I arrive home, and I creep back in the kitchen, forcing my eyes to stay open as I very carefully replace the latch. Rummaging in the dirty clothes, I pull out my dressing gown that I stored there earlier and wrap it over my dress. Just in case, it'll look like, on the surface at least, that I only popped downstairs for a little while. Maybe a midnight snack. For good measure I grab a piece of cheese out of the cool box.

Skipping the sixth stair, I climb the staircase, so sure at every step that someone will wake, someone will have noticed I'm gone. It's not until I reach my room, carefully open the door, and pull it shut behind me to lean against it with a sigh of relief, that I relax.

"Wendy. Where have you been?"

The tearful voice of my youngest brother pulls me out of my half-asleep daze, and almost causes me a most embarrassing accident for a young girl.

"Michael?" I say and creep forward, the candle in the window for Peter the only source of light in my room.

"And me." John steps around from the other side of my bed, and for the first time I remember, my brother looks a lot like my father. Stern and not about to brook any nonsense.

But my parents aren't here, which means they haven't told them. Oh, please let them not have told them.

"I wasn't feeling well, so I went for a walk." I take a few steps, take off my dressing gown and sit on the bed.

Michael climbs into my lap and hugs me, wrinkling his nose.

"You smell like old t'ings," he says.

I hug him close as I briefly remember Stephen and the way he looked so peaceful, like nothing would ever harm him again.

"Sometimes, old things smell like old things," I tease him and tickle his tummy, but not even that makes him laugh.

"I wanted hugs and you were gone," he says accusingly, poking me with his chubby little fingers. "I got worried an' came an' got John."

He pushes his bottom lip forward and turns his huge eyes up at me. Denying my little brother has never been an option and so I scoop him up in a hug and hold him close for a little while.

"We know you weren't out walking just because you didn't feel well, Wendy." John's voice eerily resembles Mother's for the interrogation tone, and I snuggle Michael while glancing over his head.

"How would you know that?" I ask softly, patting Michael's head.

"Then you've been feeling unwell an awful lot lately." John sits next to me and leans his head on my free shoulder.

It's a strange sensation to realize your brothers have been keeping tabs on you, watching your every move and you didn't notice. How do I get them to stop? What should I say to make them understand? Can I say anything?

For a few moments I gather my thoughts, trying to decide what to say. John surprises me with a surprisingly nice gesture. "We haven't told Mother and Father. We know things aren't fun for you right now. But can we help? At all? Why are you going out so much?"

I look at those eyes, so big and round and trusting behind those huge glasses. "I've been helping homeless children cross over to Neverland."

John blinks, and Michael pulls away to look at me, speaking before our brother can.

"Why didn't you tell us?" His pouty face makes me feel even worse for keeping it from them.

"Because it's not easy to do this. People think the boys have disappeared because they never return. No one really misses them like Mother and Father would us, but people do still notice they're gone." I sit Michael gently down on the bed. "So, you can't, ever, tell anyone or I'll get into trouble. That okay?"

"No." John says hotly and then looks embarrassed by his outburst. "Did you ever think we might want to see Peter? We might want to go with you?"

"I don't really get to go to Neverland, John. I'm not doing this for fun for myself. I've only been back once, very briefly. I'm getting too old." Saying it out loud makes it far too real for me, so real in fact I have to count to ten before I can speak again. "All I do is give the boys some tea to relax them, wait until Peter comes to call, and see them on their way so they can be with the others."

"With the other lost boys?" John asks, and Michael clings to my neck.

I nod. "They're all lost boys now, John."

He watches me for a while and sighs a bit. "I'll keep your secret, but you have to tell us everything about any adventures you might have without us. It's not fair that you get to leave us behind."

"Not fair!" Michael pipes in sleepily.

"It's not fair," I agree, "But their lives have been horrible, and this is their only way out."

PROPOSAL

When I arrive home on Wednesday after visiting Stepney, there are constables in our parlor. Mother ushers me through to talk to them. They're standing sort of awkwardly in the center of the room, dwarfing the petite furniture Mother keeps in there. I can hear my brothers chasing each other around upstairs and hope they haven't let anything slip.

"This is just routine, miss, you understand." The constable looks apologetic, as if he knows the boys have run away and would like for everyone stop fussing now. It's the other officer, Constable Baker. He's silent again, observing everything, watching me.

I try to shake off the itch on the back of my neck as I turn to politely address his current partner. "Any leads?"

This officer isn't wearing a badge that I can see, so I don't know his name. But his red hair and matching freckles remind me a little of Thomas. He smiles at me. "It's not really leads we're looking for. Quite certain they've just gone off on their own. We're merely following up, just in case anyone's seen anything."

I nod. "Well, I practice letters with them and tell the boys stories three days a week. Just to help them out. I don't see them outside of the home. Sometimes one or more can be sick, so...who did you say was missing?" It's amazing how easily the lie falls from my lips. I'm getting so much better at deceit, I'd almost think I was a professional.

"Stephen. About ten years old, so—" he holds his hand up about to my chest, "high. Nimble by all account."

"Oh." I frown, shake my head, and lean a hand on the back of the loveseat. "Not Stephen. He's been practicing so hard."

"Did you do any one-on-one work with any of them?" Constable Baker butts in, his strangely pale eyes piercing, as if they can look right through me and find all the layers of secrets I hide. He holds one wrist with the other hand, fingers drumming a staccato beat against his uniform.

I shake my head and then stop. "Well, I've corrected all of them and worked with them at some point. Is that what you mean?"

"No. We have a witness who thinks they saw a woman with one of the boys last night." His gaze never leaves my face.

It's difficult to resist the urge to gulp but I manage, and turn on a beatific smile for him. "I'm sorry I can't help you, but I was at home last night, sir. I am every night."

"To be honest, miss," the redhead interjects. "It's just a woman and a boy, not necessarily Stephen who was seen. People are reportin' everythin'." He scuffs the toe of his black boots against the beautiful cream rug on the floor. The stark contrast in colors sticks in my mind.

Mother pipes up, one hand on a hip, her chin jutting slightly up with pride. "She was in her room all night, constable."

Her tone is quiet, and I send thanks to my pillows for holding the shape all night long.

"You mentioned once there might be a reason for them to run?" Baker tries one more thing before leaving.

I nod my head. "Sometimes it seems like some of them are afraid of something, or someone." I shrug. "But I'm just a girl who reads them books and teaches them letters."

Constable Baker smiles. "Of course. I have to ask. You understand."

I return the smile tightly. "Of course, I understand. I wish they didn't have to run away. I'll miss the boys."

At the last I drop my voice a little, to show how sad I am. And I don't even have to pretend, because I will miss the boys. I do wish they could still be here, but they can't. They're far better off in Neverland.

~

"I'll send word to Mrs. Johnson" are mother's first words to me after the watch leave.

I turn to face her, a little bewildered. Please don't let her have convinced Father not to allow me to continue at the orphanage. It's the only thing I look forward to other than spending some time with John and Michael.

"Send word that the watch is coming?" I ask, and I'm sure the words sound confused. I am confused.

Mother shakes her head and pats me on the shoulder. "No dear. Word that you won't be there this Friday. I need you to stay home and help me with some things."

"Just this Friday though, right?" I ask, not wanting to seem like I wouldn't help my own mother.

"For now," she says and smiles tightly. I think she's aged in the last week—I swear there are more wrinkles around her eyes. "You'll be busy for the next few days. We have a lot to do to prepare for Sunday."

This time the smile is real, almost greedy. And as soon as I see the avarice in her expression, I know what Sunday will bring, even if I try to force myself into denial as she continues.

"The Davenports will be calling on Sunday. I expect you to give him another chance and put your stories behind you. Your future is what matters now."

I bristle involuntarily at the words. Stories? I want to show him up, but I have to think of a way to do it well. Now I won't even see Thomas beforehand.

"Of course, Mother," I say, and bop into a brief curtsy before leaving the room and walking upstairs. It's only when Michael tugs on my dress that I realize I've stopped on the landing. That I'm crying great hulking sobs.

"Are you hurt, Wendy?" he asks, putting up his arms to be picked up.

I don't have the heart to tell him he's getting too old for that, that he's heavier than I'd like to be carrying. There's so much innocence left wrapped around him that maybe if I pick him up and cuddle him, it'll rub off on me, make me not know things, bring back the years I'm losing and let me into Neverland.

"I'm all right, Michael. Everything will be all right." I hug him once more and help him lead me up the steps as an idea begins to form in the back of my mind.

After all—especially with how things are right now—there's no place I'd rather be than Neverland.

Mother keeps me so busy the next few days, I almost don't know what hit me. She has me fitted for a dress on Thursday, that's obviously been on order. It's beautiful, but I resent it because I know what it's for. It's similar to the pink one I wore last time I saw him, but it's blue. Mother knows I love the color, too.

We spend Friday working on the food that Joan will fetch from the market on Saturday morning. All sorts of breakfast foods, and fruits, and cakes. An amazing spread that's going to set us back a pretty penny. I wonder what my dowry is.

"What's my dowry?" I ask before I can shy away from the question.

My mother glares at me. "That's not something we discuss."

I pop a cherry into my mouth and suck around the stone. "Shouldn't I know how much I'm worth?"

I want to ask if I shouldn't know how much I am being sold for, but that sounds a little too cattle-like.

Though I should have known Mother wouldn't answer. All she does is glare at me and move to the other side of the kitchen. If the Davenports are a wealthy family, what could we possibly give them that would make his marrying me enticing?

The main thing about these days leading up to the dreaded Sunday is that Mother leaves me no time at all to sneak anywhere. It's a good thing I didn't have a boy waiting in the way-house. He'd have died of starvation by now. As it is, all I want to do is visit Thomas and feel like I have a purpose outside of being this piece of property about to be passed between families.

Dreams haven't been visiting me lately. Just visions and nightmares. All of Albert, with Thomas and Peter there and lost boys who aren't real and who dissipate as soon as I get close.

~

When Sunday finally dawns, I'm already awake. Sleep was elusive. Along with everything else.

I think the stress of this whole marriage thing is starting to get to me. I swear Stephen was in my room last night, his body strangely grey in the light of the moon, but when I turned to look at him face on, he wasn't there. Just as I was falling asleep this morning, I thought I saw Peter, but that's not possible. Neither was sleep afterward.

My dress hangs on my wardrobe, the blue shining beautifully in the morning sunlight. It's a pity how tarnished it'll be once Albert sees me in it. I've never been one to dote on dresses, but this type? I think the style truly will catch on. If it wasn't for the proposed company, I'd feel like a princess in it.

Joan brings up a very light breakfast for me. Usually I love this sort. Marmalade and some toast, a scone and a hardboiled egg, but nothing about it looks appetizing to me this morning. Mother didn't want me to have an empty stomach, yet all I smell is this stench of rotting decay, like a rat is trapped somewhere on my plate, dead and decomposing. I can barely look at the food.

I hide the piece of toast on the windowsill, hoping the birds will feast in style since I obviously can't this morning. At least that way it'll look like I ate something. Can't have Mother chastising me for yet another thing.

She's perfectly on time as she raps at the door.

"Wendy?" she asks as she pushes through without waiting for me to answer.

"In here," I murmur as I wash my face with the fresh water in my pitcher. Which reminds me, the way-house needs to be replenished shortly, or there'll be nothing to make tea for the next batch of boys.

"I wasn't expecting you to be ready to get dressed." She sounds surprised and impressed. "Excellent. We can greet them at the door together. Today is going to be a wonderful day, Wendy."

I nod at her, not trusting myself to speak. Today is going to be a beautiful example of how well I can act the perfect daughter while my insides scream quietly. This will just be temporary. There hasn't been time or means to put a plan into action, but I will figure a way out of this.

Mother is staring at me, waiting for something, so I finish drying my hands and walk toward her, fake smile fixed firmly in place. I'm quite sure she won't notice if it reaches my eyes or not. Stockings. Slip. Petticoat. Boots. Dress. Ribboned waist. I watch as my body is transformed into this young woman I don't want to be. As my mother, with brief help from Joan, does my hair up in this elaborate concoction with matching ribbon. I wonder—if I pull at one of them will the whole thing come tumbling down?

That's not the real me in the mirror. Therefore, anything I say today isn't really me speaking. I'll probably get through it if I think like that. Neverland will spit me out if it sees me looking like this. I'm not fond enough of Hook to try and side with him just because I'm old.

I'm glad Mother isn't trying to make small talk.

"There," she says as Joan scurries back to the kitchen to check on brunch. I can't help feeling a life like hers, though hard work, would probably be a lot more fun. Free to spend her own money, free to do her own thing when she can—

"Sorry?" I ask Mother, who's standing with her hands on her hips glaring at me. I missed what she said in all my contemplations.

"I gave you a compliment," she says. "You look amazing."

"Perfect." I smile and open the door, only to have Michael barrel into me.

"Wendy!"

"Watch where you're going, Michael." The impatience in my mother's voice makes me cringe, and I have to smooth the expression over so Michael doesn't get worried.

"There, there, Michael, what's wrong?" I ask and crouch down to talk to him at eye height.

"I miss you, Wendy" is all he says as he throws those pudgy arms around me and hugs me so tight it's hard to breathe. He lets go, kisses my cheek and runs back to the nursery.

Stunned, I only move because Mother bends down to pick me up from under my elbow.

"Sweet," she mutters, "I only hope he didn't have anything sticky on him."

I'm glad she can't see my face, because I stick my tongue out at her. How's that for grown up?

We make it downstairs in the nick of time for the Davenports to ring our doorbell.

Suddenly my hands sweat and I'm nervous. I don't want to do as I'm told, and as Albert enters the house I swear I can feel every single finger imprint from the other day flare to life against my skin, see every animal he ever tortured in front of me, every toy he ever destroyed. My breath comes raggedly, and I can't meet anyone's eyes.

Mrs. Davenport hugs me, and the totally unexpected maneuver has me floundering as her husband shakes my hand vigorously. He's the father, the one who's made it all right in that family. The urge to pinch his hand is almost overwhelming, but my contempt boils over and leaves me feeling so weak I'm sure I only manage to squeak out a greeting or two.

Then Albert is in front of me, and I want to cry, I want to pick up my skirts and run. I want to be invisible. When he drops down on one knee in front of me, my heart tries to escape through my throat, momentarily blocking all breath from my lungs.

He can't be. Not now, not here. I don't want any of this!

"Wendy Darling. Would you do me the honor of becoming my bride?"

I know that tone to his voice. This is a joke to him, that curl to his upper lip hides a horrible fate for me. Some cruel sort of entitlement he's been granted for whatever reason he sees fit. It's a game, something he's doing for sport, because he's a sportsman.

But my parents refuse to see that, and his have propagated it. All of the exits in my house are blocked. There is nowhere to run. There is nowhere to hide. And yet, I don't care.

I open my mouth and answer. "No."

AFTERMATH

$\mathcal{B}$ut just as I open my mouth to speak, so does my mother.

And her "Of course she'll be delighted to" completely drowns out my no, even though I didn't whisper.

Mr. Davenport shakes my father's hand and pats him on the back. Mrs. Davenport and my mother give each other ladylike hugs, and Albert stands up, a much better actor than I. He smiles, not a trace of the sadistic, mean undertones from our childhood present as he slips the ring onto my finger. I'm too shocked to take any real notice of it, only that it feels so much more like I'm being bound in irons than I ever expected. Chained to something for eternity, forced to grow up. For a few moments I dare to hope he was just playing the other day when he insisted this was for the best.

When he holds my hand, he squeezes so hard, I'm sure there'll be a hand imprint. But his face never changes expression—one of rapt happiness as he leans in to kiss my cheek.

"I heard your actual answer. Don't worry, I'll make sure you get what you need," he whispers into my ear, and his hot breath makes my skin crawl.

Mother is watching us, a crease in her brow. Maybe she just saw all the color drain from my face? I wonder if she's worried.

Our parents are busy talking amongst themselves, and I overhear snippets about a grand wedding from our mothers. I really hope those are tears in my eyes, and that I haven't started to twitch. The thought makes me laugh, I can't help it. Such a happy sound for a torturous occasion.

"At least you're laughing." Albert's voice is soft and sibilant, and surprised me because I didn't see his lips move through the fake smile. I freeze, unsure of how to respond.

"Perfect." He says and slips his hands around my shoulders, digging his fingertips in while trying to make it look as if he's helping me relax. "You'll have to get used to a real household. No time to weave stories, I'm afraid."

"We have a real household." I ignore the rest of his insults in the face of his insult to Joan.

He scoffs at me. "You're not serious. You have one maid, who cooks for you."

"The boys have a tutor, and Joan is worth three of any other maid." I can feel my face getting flushed as the anger rises in me.

"Now, now, Wendy. Please don't make a scene. In the end you'll realize your parents only did this for your well-being." He squeezes my shoulders again and I gasp a little despite my best efforts.

"Good." He carries on. "You'll be the perfect wife."

"Perfect?" I manage to grind out between teeth clenched so hard in a fake smile it pains my jaw. Not like his fingertips hurt, but still.

"Presentable. Pleasant. With enough to do that you won't be able to fabricate things." He nods over to his mother. "You know my mother knows all about the stories, don't you?"

My stomach twists as the truth about this arrangement, sinks into place. My blood runs cold at the thought that someone else could want to inflict the same type of misery on another. My fondness for his mother fades. "Makes sense."

Albert's smile thins, and this slightly mad twinkle enters his eyes. "Good."

The rest of the day is a blur, and I barely keep it together. I can't prove a thing about him if the bruises are discarded. Nothing. From a distance it looks like he's always being nice to me. He should be performing Shakespeare in the park. Every time I open my mouth to say something, it's like he knows, as if he can read my mind.

"Your father's a hard worker, Wendy. This is good for all of us. I'm really hoping you'll end up happy." He always lingers on that last phrase, working it over with his snake-like manner, boring his horribly cruel eyes into my soul.

Maybe if I get run over by horses, I'll be horribly disfigured and we can back out without Father losing face? That'd be so mean for the driver though, and for the horses. There has to be some valid option for me.

"Does next spring sound good to you, Wendy?" My mother's voice snaps me out of my inner thoughts.

I look at her, back at my father, open my mouth to speak a vehement *no* again, but catch Albert's expression to the side of me. He'd ruin my father, my whole family. The boys would have to live in a one-bedroom little apartment with my parents, and my mother would never forgive me. A rash plan isn't a plan at all.

"Naturally," I say, which in my mind isn't a yes or a no, it's a delay, because I need to delay this in my head until I can figure something out. End of summer is about nine months away. Just after my sixteenth birthday. Eleven months away. Eleven months.

Someone help me.

~

*W*hen I pull myself out of bed on Monday morning, my hands are shaking. Probably because I've not been sleeping. Again. Really have to do something to change that. I pull on the closest thing at hand. A nicely striped day dress, and grab the matching hat. On the way downstairs I avoid the dining room and exit through the kitchen where I take a cup of tea and gulp it down, dashing out of the doors before anyone can catch me.

Except once I'm outside, I realize I forgot the breadbasket. At least no one else is in there when I grab that and exit a little more sedately this time. There's a ring on my finger. A pretty little dark red ruby surrounded by lots of diamonds. It weighs my hand down like a boulder. Maybe it'll let me sink to the bottom if I throw myself in a river.

Perhaps I can sell it somewhere you sell such things and afford to run away? A thousand thoughts flit through my mind, but I didn't want Mother and Father to stop me from going to the orphanage. This morning, I need to be there. Today is one of my three days. I will be there.

Even as I drop the bread off and head into the living area, there's only one thought on my mind. Thomas. I need to see Thomas. Excruciating as it is now, I need to share something with my only true friend, the one person I know will listen to me and not call me a liar. The only person I can trust here.

My skin itches all over, as if it wants me to scratch it right off, and I'm sorely tempted to do so. The sea of faces in front of me blurs and I choose to just tell them a tale, one I know so well, one I wish I'd never left the confines of. It's easier to speak about something to do with Neverland, to recount the tales, the battles, the fears. To enjoy the rapt attention of all these boys even though most of them have heard it umpteen times before.

It's relaxing in a way no one can ever help me with.

I have this horrible feeling that my days of coming here are numbered. They definitely won't outlast my wedding in the spring. I'll be taken away, housed somewhere I'm unfamiliar with, and tasked with all these duties I can't even begin to understand. They want to distract me from the stories they think I tell, to keep me from revisiting Neverland. The panic starts to set back in as the younger boys filter out to have lunch. I've not seen Thomas since I got here, and I don't want to leave before I have.

He'll fix things, won't he? Doesn't he always fix things for the boys? Surely, he can think of some amazing plan to smuggle me out of this nightmare? But the room is empty, and this chair seems impossibly large right now. I pull my legs up under my skirt and latch my hands around my knees. So much easier to just bury my face and cry this way. My own little cocoon where no one can see what goes on inside.

I'm not sure how much time passes, but the moment his hand rests on my shoulder, I begin to relax. I know it's him, even though he's not yet said a word and I don't care that he shouldn't be touching me. At least he's not bruising and threatening me. Even the tears stop flowing, but I don't want to lift my head and look at him with a face reddened by sadness.

Thomas's voice is soothing and tempered when he speaks. "I'm so sorry, Wendy. I couldn't get here earlier. They were questioning the older boys in connection with the disappearances."

I forget my resolution not to look at him with a tear-stricken face and stare at him. I'd completely forgotten about the disappearances, and the questions, and all the boys we'd saved.

"Is everything all right?" I ask, barely recognizing my own voice through the thickness of too much crying.

He nods, and kneels down in front of my chair. It's so different from the way Albert did it that I want to cry again. Thomas takes my hands in his and opens his mouth to speak, but stops short and looks at my fingers. I can see his brain working, his eyes fixated on the blood red stone, and I wait, because I don't know what to say, how I can explain it any better than its existence does.

"Already?" he asks, a different tone to his voice than I expected.

"Yesterday." I'm proud of how calmly I say the word, because my mind is still flitting from one possible solution to the next, addressing them, dismissing them and trying to figure out ways out of this.

"But I thought we had more time." He's not really looking at me though, as his words echo what's in my own mind so beautifully.

Sometimes I think he knows me a little too well. His thoughts weren't finished, so I wait, gripping his hands tightly with my own, scared that he won't have a solution, that I will realize any solution he offers isn't viable.

"When?" he asks instead of how long we have. It's kind of sweet but misleading at the same time. I'll be so busy I doubt—

Breathing deep, I answer. "Eleven months."

"But you'll be older then." He says it carefully. "An adult. You can't wait that long. It won't work."

"What won't work?" And I think I know what he's going to say, because it's the only option I see as truly open to me right now. I'm just not sure how open it is, how realistic I'm being. Could I really do it? Could we really do it?

Thomas smiles at me. "I know you haven't wanted to take me before, and I don't quite understand why, but if there's nothing here for you, if there's nothing here for either of us anymore. Why don't we go to Neverland together?"

The hopeful look in his eyes sparks feelings in my chest I've guarded with jealousy. I lean forward and rest my head against his, happy to feel the warmth of his breath across my cheek, the gentle way he holds my hands, the thrill of knowing I'm not the only one who feels this way. This is nothing like Albert, nothing like the nightmare I'm being consigned to grow old with.

"If I'm going with you, taking you to Neverland is no problem at all." I say it quietly, and hope he understands what I mean. The fierce hug I get in return tells me he probably does. It's a relief.

Pulling back, I hold him at arm's length. "I'm scared though. I'm getting older so fast, I'm not sure they'll still consider me a child. I might be too old already."

Thomas laughs and pulls me into a hug. "Then we'll join Captain Hook and hunt down that croc!"

The laughter aches, but is freeing. There's so much to organize, so much to do. I don't know how to work around things like my brothers. Should we take them?

"We need to do this now." Thomas echoes my own thoughts on the matter.

"Thursday night?" I ask, quite certain I can make it that far.

He smiles at me. "Thursday night it is. Will you be back on Wednesday?" He asks the question, glancing around as he does so.

"I'll fight for it. Try my best to be here."

He nods, and reluctantly lets go of my hand. "I have to go help with the end of lunch."

"I know. I'll be back." And I will be. As I watch him walk away I worry for a few moments. Neverland is forever, where we'll never come back from, where we'll never grow old, where we'll always be just as we are now. Is that what he truly wants? Is that what I truly want?

What I don't want is to end up as Albert's bride. Maybe I should start there instead.

Which means I need to speak to Peter.

MACHINATIONS

$\mathcal{M}$other is waiting for me when I get home. I can tell as soon as I set foot in the house that she's unimpressed. But to be fair, I was fairly certain of that before I got anywhere near the house.

"Why on earth did you go to the orphanage this morning? Your fiancé stopped by and was chagrined that you weren't at home."

Though I feel a slight stab of elation at the fact that I missed one of Albert's visits, I take a deep breath before replying, so as not to show it. Can't have Mother catching on and realizing what's going to happen.

"They are a prior arrangement, Mother. What sort of wife would I be if I backed out of previous engagements where people depend on me?"

Mother blinks, and I resist the urge to leer at her with a triumphant grin. Instead, I hope I'm keeping my expression neutral and pleasant. It works if I try to focus on one of the entryway tiles.

"I see your point. You may have to stop working there at the end of the summer though, so we have enough time to devote to the planning and arrangement of your wedding." She begins to walk away only to turn back around again. "What days do you go? So, I can let Albert know not to call those mornings."

I smile. Fake smile. Forced smile. "Mondays. Wednesdays. Fridays."

Mother knows the days. She's the one who restricted them in the first place.

But she smiles at me. "Thank you. And please, try and make Michael understand that you're not abandoning them, you're just moving onto a new and better stage in your life."

I watch her leave, wishing my eyes could throw daggers at her back. It's typical of her to leave explaining anything if not to both boys, at least to Michael. It wouldn't be that difficult to take them with me. It's not like Mother has time for them. I'm sure I could manage it. But they don't have the options I do. There is more they can do with their lives here, indeed, they're expected to achieve more than I am.

I begin to trudge upstairs, barely lifting my skirts enough not to trip over them. I breathe deeply and go through my options. I can marry Albert and live miserably ever after as a piece of display material subject to his temper and threats, devoid of my stories of our time in Neverland.

Second, I could run away with the ring and try to sell it and set myself up somewhere with minimal funds and no real skills to take into any sort of workplace. Although, I guess I know how to help prepare breakfast in a home, or how to look after small children. This option leaves my family in the lurch, and doesn't guarantee me any sort of freedom or happiness. I'll grow old, wither and die. That option is depressing.

Thirdly, I could see if Neverland will take me back. I'm borderline too old, although not much older than Peter was when he came to get me, so maybe I can still sneak in under the line. If I choose this option and leave the ring behind, I'm sure the repercussions for my family would be less. This ring is valuable, and not selling it will make it easier for my father to dig himself out of any debt he holds to the Davenports. In fact, if I remember correctly from my lessons that halted not too long ago, my parents will be the ones paying for the wedding, and providing the dowry. So, option three not only lets me get to Neverland and essentially live forever as I am now, never grow up, never grow old—it also gives my parents the best possible outcome that doesn't involve using me to elevate the family standing.

Idiosyncrasies aside, now that I've reasoned things through, my stomach doesn't feel like it's tied in knots. Granted, something is still holding me back, tugging at the back of my mind. *Neverland is forever* it whispers to me. And I know it is, and always should be. Should have been when we visited as a group.

Maybe if I could turn back time and make us all stay. I'd had to convince the boys we needed to return home. But maybe crying would have been better for my parents in the long run.

Packing. Will I need to pack? No one there ever seemed to have too many clothes or shoes, or a hat in sight. My door is slightly ajar, and I push into it without a thought.

A catapult launches itself at my legs and clings hard and fast wailing at me. Nanna is curled up on my rug, and John is hugging one of the pillows on my bed, trying his best to glare at me, but the reddened rings around his eyes give away that he's been crying.

Disentangling Michael from my legs is a chore, but I manage it eventually and he clings to my neck instead. With a sigh, I sit down next to John, wishing I was in my little blue smock, and easy flat shoes, with no stupid hat on my head. At first, I don't know what to say to them, I don't know how to console them. They've obviously heard I'll be getting married and moving away. That I'll come back to see them when I can, but likely, all too soon have children of my own.

Children of my own.

I can't do that. I'm still a child myself. This whole scenario is ridiculous.

"What did you overhear?" I ask softly, wanting to make sure I don't upset them more than they already are. But just as I feared, John heard pretty much everything.

"Albert. Marriage. Eleven Months. Moving away from us forever."

I cringe at the accuracy.

"You not really gonna marry that man, Wendy? Are you?" Michael rubs his hands over his eyes, brushing away the tears that threatened to overwhelm his tiny face.

There's a split second to make the decision. A split second to decide what I'm going to do, and who needs to know, and who will be coming with me.

"No." I shake my head. "I don't love him. I don't even like him. And love is sort of a central theme when you get married."

Michael smiles. "Like Daddy loves Mommy."

Strange how astute little boys' perceptions are. He knows Daddy loves Mommy and not the other way around.

"Exactly," I say.

"But if you're not marrying him, what are you going to do?" John caught on.

He's smart. He's always been smart. But will taking him with me really be in his best interests? Surely here he can get a far better future than I can even dream of, what with his brain, gender, and resources.

In for a penny... "I'm going to talk to Peter and see if I can go to Neverland."

I wait for a few moments as they both look at me, mouths agape. And then the question comes, as if out of one mouth, one mind, and one heart.

"Can we come too?"

It's such a conflicted feeling to watch the way my little brothers idolize me. I've told them this secret, and they know to never tell anyone else about Neverland. Ever. It was part of our deal when we first visited there, part of our little pact to return home. But they know it. How amazing it is, how freeing. They can fly there, have parties, play with pirate swords and find treasure.

Sort of like a never-ending story book.

I wish I could take all the boys. My brothers, and the little ones at Stepney Causeway. But I know there's not enough tea for that. Though there's probably enough for all four of us, there's just not enough for the rest. I might have to bring fresh water and some kindling on Thursday.

My mind won't stop flitting, and shying away from answering the question my brothers ask. In their mind's it's harmless. But I can see the ramifications so much clearer now. What their possible futures might be here, so much better than never growing up. They might achieve great things.

"We'll see. You're still so young, maybe Peter can come back and get you later."

John thinks about this for a very long while and finally nods his head. "Okay. I think it'd be better if we came now, easier not to say anything. But I understand."

Sometimes I think John has already grown up more than I have.

I ruffle his hair, and hug Michael close. "Don't worry. I'll never let any harm come to you."

~

I pull two of my nice, new-styled dresses into a bag. It's difficult to squash them down, and fit a smock in there with them, but I'll have to change at the way-house. Even though I'm planning on trying to wear my nice flat, sensible shoes with whatever I wear to get there. Avoiding the watch is all about appearances. No one will suspect me if I walk with purpose in well-to-do clothes. Especially if we appear to be adults.

The watch is forever vigilant, especially with six boys gone from the home. It's frightening to think that six people could simply disappear, but because they don't have true family, no one really notices. People at the home noticed, but there's such a high turnover there, it's almost like just another day.

An unexpected knock at my door sends me momentarily into panic as I stuff the bag into my closet. Mother pushes in just in time to see me pushing some of my hair behind my ear, and I school my face into mild surprise to see her. Or I think raising an eyebrow and opening my mouth slightly depicts surprise. "Mother?"

"Mrs. Davenport will be here for tea in a short while. We need to discuss some wedding things." She looks me up and down, her lips pursed slightly frowning her face. "You dressed yourself this morning?"

I'm unsure of her tone, but hazard a guess.

"Yes."

"Excellent, Wendy. I thought you were going to make things difficult. It won't be so bad, you'll see. You're not used to him yet. You're just exaggerating his behaviour." She walks over and hugs me tightly.

I've never wanted to have a dagger in my hand so much. Without her to make my life this miserable, I think I could even be happy accepting the fate of growing up. Hatred grips a hold of my heart and digs into it. People say hating something takes far too much energy. I'm of two minds about that at the moment. For the first time in my life, I refuse to hug her back.

After a moment she pulls away, puzzlement in her eyes, like she doesn't know what to think of it. "Wendy. Are you all right?"

I have to say something. Just like I wouldn't stand idly by on Hook's ship. Shouldn't she be proud of the pride I take in myself, in being my own person? "You know very well I didn't accept his proposal, and you know just as well he's not just acting out."

She steps back, shaking her head and refuses to meet my gaze.

"So, to answer your question, Mother. No, I'm not all right."

"It's done now, Wendy." She motions to the ring on my finger, and I feel trapped again, but just for a moment. "You'll be taken care of."

Slowly, I reach down and remove it, holding it out to her. "You mean this? If you like it so much, you can have it. I hate it. it weighs me down."

My room is suddenly far too small as she stands there gaping at me. I hold my head up high and continue to watch her, waiting for some sort of sign other than the bewilderment and recognition spreading slowly across her face.

I push past her and begin to open the door, when I hear what sounds amazingly like a sob. I turn, hand still on the handle, and gaze at my mother. At least I think she's my mother. Maybe it's a changeling, which might explain a few things. But she's crouched against the ground, one hand steadying herself while the other covers her eyes.

It's strange, but I only feel a slight tug of remorse. But I do wait, because I sense she wants to say something.

"I'm sorry," she mumbles. "You don't understand."

Choking down my anger, I bite out my words. "No. You're right. I don't understand."

"We've fought for everything so hard for so long. We just can't keep taking care of you the way you need it." She looks at me, tears streaming down her face, and I think it's the first time in the last few years my mother isn't pretending to be anyone but who she is.

"Fighting so hard for so long gives you the right to sell me off to the best offer just because I'm difficult?" I ask it quietly, because I need to know. I need to understand if that's how things work in this world, if this is what's expected of everyone or just of me.

She pushes herself back up to standing, but the confidence is gone, the bravado has disappeared. Her shoulders sag, and her face contorts through pinched brows, through frowns, and finally her expression simply slackens. "It's the way everything is done in these circles. We've secured you a future, with no questions, with no hardships. You need this."

It's the answer I dreaded, but also the answer I needed. I walk over to her and give her a hug, because I feel sorry that she's already so grown up that there's no more hope for her, or my father. It's a tight, emotional grip, and Mother hugs back so hard I think I feel my spine pop once. When I pull away, I wipe the tears off her face.

"I can't pretend to understand, because I couldn't do what you've done. But I'll assure you that at the end of all of this, it'll be all right." Because it will. I now know without a shadow of a doubt, that this world is not one I'll ever want to grow old in.

NEVERLAND

Sneaking out of the house has never been so harrowing or so scary as tonight. I hold my bag in one hand, while Michael clutches my other in his and drags his teddy along-side of him. It's been over a year since we were in Neverland together. All of us. John has his nose in the air, chin jutting forward, showing us and the rest of the world how unafraid he is. I'd believe him if his knees weren't knocking together.

"You can still change your mind, John," I tell him as we walk along Commercial to meet Thomas at the corner of Belgrave. Maybe I should be being the better person, the one who acts like the adult and is stern with my brother. But I can't do it. In the end, I don't want us to be separated either. It's only a pity we had to leave the dog at home. I'm just not sure if the Neverland effect will work on her too.

John shakes his head and gives me his bravest smile.

"You know we've always wanted to stay in Neverland," he says and pushes his glasses up on his nose.

There's still light in the sky as it begins to turn all different shades, a kaleidoscope of color on the horizon. The one truly beautiful thing about where we live. Thomas is waiting on the corner, and I can feel the adrenaline pounding in my stomach. I keep expecting to hear

Mother or Father's footsteps behind us as they discover all that's in our beds are pillows shaped to look like a body at a quick glance. That they'll realize I've left my ring and a note explaining not to worry about us, that we're going to be fine. It's exhilarating, yet sort of scary.

"Hey." Thomas greets us as we arrive, and falls into step.

"This is Thomas. He's the one whose idea it was to help those other boys."

I turn to Thomas and hug him quickly, not losing stride as he takes my bag from me.

"This is John and Michael," I add almost as an afterthought.

He smiles at them, a big grin, just like the ones the boys at the home fall in love with—it's the reason everyone trusts him. Part of the reason I never wanted to take him to Neverland. I don't want to share him with others. I don't want anyone else to have a claim to his time. But Albert left me no choice. I will not be subjected to that for the rest of my life.

My nerves get the better of me as we pass Troon Street where the lamps are being lit. I swear I can hear someone walking behind us and my heart sits in my throat. It's been in there an awful lot lately. I stop for a moment, and Michael almost stumbles. But I pull him into my lap as if I'm fixing his shoe, and glance behind me as I stand back up.

There's just one person a fair distance behind us, walking in a way that tugs at my memory, but from the corner of my eyes I can see they're in a work smock. As much as I try, I realize I must be being paranoid. Mother and Father haven't followed us. One of them would have called out to us already. It's just a coincidence.

Relief floods through me and all I can think of is getting to the way-house. It's a good night, where this street is just outside of the watch changes and patrols at this particular time. Michael squeezes my hand and I smile down at him.

"We're going to see Peter, Wendy?" His eyes shine brightly as he looks up at me, and I laugh.

"Yes, Michael. We're going to see Peter and all the lost boys."

"We're going to be lost boys." Thomas says, and for a moment I'm cold enough to shiver. I shake it off, but it lingers and I'm not sure how on such a warm and beautiful evening.

I think the excitement is getting to me. I watch as John and Michael interact easily with Thomas and realize finally that I made the right choice. I'm not sure if we'll all need the tea, but I know Thomas will. I have a glass jar of fresh water in my bag to make sure there's enough in case the boys decide they want some too. It won't hurt to give them it if they want it. But Thomas has never been, so he has to have it.

I lead them around the house at the back and Michael begins to cough as we pass over the coal cellar grate. He looks up at me, tears welling in his eyes. "Horrible smell, Wendy."

"I'm sorry," I say and mean it. "That room is dark as night and I can't bring myself to try and clean it, so it just stays shut."

"Will it smell this bad down there?" Thomas looks a little green around the gills and I laugh.

"No, it's not that bad down there. Just musty, and a bit fetid."

He smiles with relief, and the eagerness leaks back into his expression as I unlatch the door. Walking through to the main hall, I realize the setting sun has left not only red, but orange swooshes of color for us, painting the floors and even some of the walls as if blood were flung onto them. For a moment it shifts, revealing a strange hue of grey, like a cracked image of one of those new photograph things gone wrong. I blink, and it's bathed in blood again.

"This is great," I hear John saying. "Why don't we just stay here?"

I shake my head. "Father's bank owns this house. Can't seem to sell it."

"Good reason," Thomas mutters as I walk to the cellar door.

"It's dark down here," I say apologetically. "Just let me head down and light a few candles so it's easier to walk down the stairs.

The smell is worse than I remember when I enter the cellar. We only need to put up with it for a few more hours. After a while it'll fade away, but I'm really starting to hate rats. I clear out the old nubs by the light of a new candle, and set some more down on the makeshift ledge near the cushion couch.

"Come on down," I call as I set up the kindling to boil enough water for us all.

I hear two sets of feet clomping down the stairs, and look up to see Thomas carrying Michael. The sight makes me smile. If only Thomas had been Albert, or vice versa, however would have made it work. But he's not. He's Thomas, and I think I like that better.

"If you sit in the cushions, know that they suck you in. It's difficult to get up." I feel the warning is appropriate.

The water comes to a boil as the boys dart around pretending to be pirates on a ship escaping a crocodile. It's cute to see them reliving our adventure, introducing a new friend to the same one.

I swirl the leaves in the teapot first and pour Thomas's cup before I try to speak up, but for a few moments it's difficult. Do we really want to do this? This level of permanence away from a world we've always known? Or do I go back home, and remain as a tool of whatever it is I'll become?

My resolve shifts back in place and I smile up at the boys. "Thomas. You need to drink this. I'm not sure if the boys do, since they've been there, and I didn't have to take it to go back, but this is for anyone new wanting to go."

John stands up. "I'll have a sip! Can't let Thomas drink alone now."

He grins, and his lanky form looks all sorts of more grown up than I remember. For a moment I hesitate pouring him a small serving, but I relent and hand him a smaller cup.

Michael walks over to John and sniffs the contents, crinkling his nose up.

"Smells sweet. Can I have a taste?" But the moment it hits his lips, he pulls back, pushing his tongue out of his mouth and making horrible expressions with his face. "I like not drinking dat."

We all laugh, and then we sit in and wait for Peter to come get us.

The wait is surprisingly short considering how long I've had to wait before. But Michael is asleep against my shoulder, and I motion to Peter to be quiet.

John and Thomas lay in the cushions, grinning from ear to ear.

Peter shrugs and points at us, raising his eyebrows. It's all I can do not to laugh. Laughing will wake up Michael and that will never be good. He's a very grumpy waker.

"We all need to leave."

He points at me, so I nod.

For a few moments he watches me, crossing his arms and tapping his foot. Then he sighs and shrugs.

"Very well," Peter says. "We'll see how this works."

His voice is softer than I've ever heard it, and I'm grateful. I can't wait for Thomas to experience flying, and Neverland first hand.

Tink flies through the window slit and gasps at me. She places tiny fists on her hips and glares at me, lifting one hand to shake a fist and point to all of the boys. I'm not sure why she's so angry, but I hold up my free hand to interrupt her tiny chiming sounds.

"We have to leave." I say. "Forever."

Her eyes narrow, and she nods once, allowing Peter to grab her and shake dust on us all. The exit is tough for Thomas, but we manage, I only hope the pixie magic keeps us safe in the night sky. Away from prying eyes, away from our futures of uncertainty and the family we leave behind.

Morose though I feel for a few moments, there isn't time to stay like that. The wind through my hair, even as I carefully carry my sleeping brother evokes feelings I thought I'd left behind. And the sight of the islands, the water and the campfires as we land is some of the best coming home I've ever had.

There is food a plenty. I'm not sure how they come about all of it, but the fruits and the sweet pies, are amazing. At least I think so now, before having to eat it forever, but I'll worry about that later. Laying Michael down gently, I stroke his hair back from his eyes. He looks so peaceful, if a little pale. He's always been able to sleep through anything. John coughs violently a couple of times, but otherwise he and Thomas appear dazed. Maybe it's the tea that makes the eyes glaze over like that. I've noticed it in all of the boys. John did insist, after all. He needs to take the consequences like a big boy. I can't baby him here, but I can be his sister.

Joshua and Tybalt wave at me from a distance where they sit gathered with the other boys. All together. Like I promised. The tears of happiness begin to overwhelm me. They're happy. We did it. We took them away from their house of horrors.

"Do you want to dance?" Peter asks me and I nod, taking his hand and swirling away with him. He twirls me around in the air, higher and higher for a few rounds making me laugh breathlessly.

But then his expression grows serious. "Why did you need to escape, Wendy? What happened?"

It's odd to see Peter so solemn. I don't think I've ever seen him serious, not even when fighting Hook.

"They wanted me to grow up. Now. Not when I would, but now. They wanted to marry me off, to make me responsible for others—to a horrible, cruel and nasty man." I look away, down to where my brothers and Thomas sit contentedly watching the lost boys' shenanigans.

I've never been that good with heights and should have known better than to look down. The ground shifts beneath me, from colors and fires and merriment so far below, back to dirt and rock with strange grey appendages dancing into view. My chest heaves with exertion, sweat beads my brow, and my feet stumble. I shake my head and Peter's arm steadies me.

The view below snaps back into place and I smile. "I had to escape. I had to come to Neverland so I can stay just as I am now. So we all can. They deserve that at least."

I can't take my eyes off Thomas as Peter lowers us both gently and gives me a very brief hug. "We'll all be this way now. They all will. The only thing that will tell is the passage of time."

"What?" I say, shaking my head again, bringing my focus back to Peter, unsure of what my ears think they heard.

Peter laughs. "The lost boys. They will always be lost, always be dead and gone to the world they came from." He spreads his arm and twirls around, and around, faster and faster until my eyes hurt with the change of scenes around him. In and out of black and white, dancing with macabre visions of things I can't grasp. Where the blood lit great rooms snap into focus as quickly as Thomas lying on the cushions and staring at me with those glassy eyes.

The spinning stops just as Peter does, and Thomas and John sit near the campfire, smiling in a strange way at with other, with the others. Even if I strain to hear, there is nothing to listen to as the lost boys dance around their campfire, mouths moving in mimicry of speech to one another, music suddenly silent.

My head hurts, and a stench reaches my nose. I wonder if Michael soiled himself in his sleep. Isn't he too old for that? Isn't the smell familiar?

It's overpowering, and my head begins to spin. Suddenly Michael is coughing and tugging at my dress, and I feel like the smoke of the fires is in my throat, trying to choke me with its density, or maybe just black out the smell.

"Wendy?" His voice sounds panicked, teary. "Wendy, I feel so sick."

The coughing and spluttering continues, and I hear it coming from further away too.

I look down at where his pudgy little hands grip into my skirt, both of them. He lost Teddy somewhere along the way. But looking down at him shifts the colors away and the dank and dirty floor of the cellar spins into view for a moment. Reaching down, I pull him up to me, and the colors seep back into my sight.

Something is wrong. Dreadfully wrong.

Michael clutches at me, coughing, sniffling, and retching up bile. I hug him, hold him, unsure of how to handle this. I didn't realize lost boys could get sick.

"Wendy," he sobs into my neck. "What's wrong with John and Thomas?"

I freeze. John and Thomas are fine. But when I look over, a piece of the sky falls, crashing into the ocean, revealing the slitted window we flew through. I take a step back and try to orientate myself, searching for Peter, but he's nowhere to be found.

When I finally find my brother and Thomas, they're lying on a pile of dirty, faded cushions near the campfire that flickers in and out. John is breathing heavily, his head beaded with sweat, his eyes unfocused as he coughs up bile again. Thomas's glassy eyes stare at the ceiling, his mouth open ever so slightly, with no trace of joy or a smile in the expression.

"Oh no," I murmur and take a few steps before stumbling to my knees in front of them, clutching Michael to my chest. "What does this mean?"

I ask it of nothing, because the lost boys are gone and the rest of Neverland is slowly breaking apart. Thomas's hand is limp, and John's is cold and clammy. The intelligence seeps from my brother's eyes to be replaced by a cloudiness I don't understand.

As the rest of the world starts to crumble, I hear the impossible. My mother's voice, my father's cry.

"Oh no, Wendy. What have you done?"

The rest of Neverland crashes down.

~

As the pieces shatter silently around me, a new light shines on the cellar. I never realized how dank it was, how unappealing, how shabby, and dilapidated. The cushions on the floor have faded so much they're grey, much like my brother's pallor as he lays there staring at nothing his chest heaving sporadically. And Thomas...oh, Thomas.

A sob hitches in my throat and matches pace with the quiet crying of Michael still clutched to my chest. I see my parents and shadows of men behind them, and watch as my father puts a handkerchief over his nose to block out the smell before he starts searching for its source.

Memories snap into place. Of Albert fingers squeezing my hand in reassurance. Of his concern when I almost fell out of the horseless carriage. Of my mother's worry over my daytime nightmares. And of the woman following us and her familiarity, of the sudden realization that it was Joan.

It's the only thing that explains my parents being here. I think there's someone else here, but I can't focus on them. We were so careful. I was always so careful. No one should have found any of us.

Ever.

Never.

More distant memories filter back into my mind like a puzzle suddenly finding its pieces. Of James, David, Tybalt, Henry, Joshua, and Stephen all drinking tea. Then laying down in the cushions and finding it so difficult to get up, because they couldn't, wouldn't ever again.

A tear rolls down my cheek and I realize Michael is sluggish. He had a taste of the drink, and he's so much smaller.

"No," I whisper and hold him in front of me, making sure he's really still all right.

"Wendy," he says, pitifully weak.

I stand up and turn, only to realize my father is prying open the coal cellar.

"No, don't!" I want to call out, because I know with sheer certainty that in there, amongst the coal, in the overwhelming darkness, is my Neverland. And my dear, dear rats.

But he doesn't hear my whispered plea, and the stench that rolls out makes my mother gag and retch in a corner. Her face is pale, eyes bewildered, as if she doesn't know what to make of it. My limbs won't move properly, and I watch in slow motion as my father and Constable Baker take a lamp into the coal cellar. I can hear cries of shock, of utter disbelief at the bodies piled in there. I remember them sort of, carrying them there, or carrying them to bed, to rest, to be with the others like I promised.

All the things running through my head when I meant to bring them to safety, truly meant well. And finally of Tinkerbell and Peter. Did they really exist? And what about the tea?

The tea I should have drunk.

I'm supposed to be dead.

If I was dead, John wouldn't be dying.

If I was dead, Thomas would still be alive.

I set Michael down at Mother's feet, but she doesn't notice. He clings to her leg and I touch her arm.

"He's sick. Take care of him yourself, for once, please."

Her eyes don't focus on me, but she bends down to pick up her only healthy son and cradles him, choking back sobs. I can hear my father's distress, but I know what I have to do now. With sudden clarity, I know where I have to go.

I drink what's left of the cool, sickeningly bitter-sweet tea in three huge gulps and lie down next to my brother and Thomas.

After all, this is what I meant to do all along.

Find my own Neverland.

AFTERWORD

I would like to take the chance to acknowledge that gaslighting, abuse, mental illness, and suicide are very serious issues.

Often these issues hang over heads of people we know, and think we know well. Please, if someone you love shows signs of experiencing any of the above, reach out to them.

If you are experiencing the above, please know that there are people who care, and resources to help you. I've gathered a few links for this purpose:

https://www.thehotline.org/what-is-gaslighting/

https://www.thehotline.org/is-this-abuse/

https://ncadv.org/get-help

https://www.domesticshelters.org/

https://www.nami.org/Find-Support

National Suicide Prevention Lifeline Call 1-800-273-8255

Available 24 hours everyday

ACKNOWLEDGMENTS

I'm not going to write a huge list here. This story is very close to my heart, sort of a pet project. It also caused me some severe setbacks when I was told it was the worst thing I'd ever written, and would never sell. I spiraled for years because of this, but I've come out the other side stronger for the struggle.

I love this book, and I want to thank the people who never gave up on it, or on me.

Jami & Owen - because always

Andrew

Heather C.

Kylie

Heather

And those that encouraged me after the fact, who loved the concept, who begged to read it, who encouraged me to put it out there:

Nick

Evan

Drew

ABOUT THE AUTHOR

KT Hanna has such a love for words, a single one can spark entire worlds.

Born in Australia, she met her husband in a computer game, moved to the U.S.A. and went into culture shock. Bonus? Not as many creatures specifically designed to kill you.

KT creates science-fiction, fantasy, and LitRPG like it's going out of style, with a dash of horror for fun! She freelance edits for Chimera Editing, plays computer games, and chases her daughter, husband, corgis, cats, and snake.

No, she doesn't sleep. She is entirely powered by the number 2, caffeine, Chipotle, and sarcasm.